Garth Jennings has directed many music videos and commercials as one third of the production company Hammer & Tongs. His work includes videos for Blur, Radiohead, Beck, Fatboy Slim and Vampire Weekend.

He is the director of three feature films: *The Hitchhiker's Guide to the Galaxy* (2005); *Son of Rambow* (2007), for which he also wrote the screenplay; and Golden Globe nominated *Sing* (2016), a feature-length animated film with an all-star cast, from the studio that created *Despicable Me*. He has also written *The Wildest Cowboy*, a picture book, for Macmillan Children's Books.

GARTH JENNINGS

THE DEADLY 7

MACMILLAN CHILDREN'S BOOKS

For Oscar

First published 2015 by Macmillan Children's Books

This abridged edition published 2019 by Macmillan Children's Books
an imprint of Pan Macmillan
20 New Wharf Road, London N1 9RR
Associated companies throughout the world
www.panmacmillan.com

ISBN 978-1-5098-8764-4

1 3 5 7 9 8 6 4 2

A CIP catalogue record for this book is available from
the British Library.

Printed and bound by CPI Group (UK) Ltd, Croydon CR0 4YY

WARNING:

Before you begin reading this book I must offer you a word of warning.

You know there will be monsters, but there are other creatures lurking within these pages that are so creepy, ghoulish and downright weird they might well put you off your dinner tonight, especially if you are eating fish.

That's not all. Along with travelling to peculiar places, learning extraordinary secrets and witnessing some very silly behaviour, there will also be moments that might scare you right out of your pants, which is why I strongly advise that you read this book with a spare pair close at hand.

You have been warned . . .

THE SLIPPERY GIANT

You may have heard it said that the eyes are the windows to the soul, and if that's true then these were the eyes of a man whose soul had packed its bags and gone on holiday. These ghoulish eyeballs didn't appear to have any iris at all, just a tiny black pupil in the middle of each bulging white orb. There was no sign of life (let alone a soul) behind them, and yet the body, this enormous, pink-skinned body, was marching along the beach at great speed. The man was as tall as a basketball player but didn't look as if he had ever played sport. His flabby chest and round belly bulged out of an open stripy shirt and his skin looked very strange indeed. The idea is to rub sun cream into your skin until it has been absorbed. This man had clearly applied so much that his skin had refused to absorb any more of it, so the stuff just lay there in great white swirls on his ever-so-pink flesh.

Carrying this enormous body along the beach were two skinny legs that ended in an entirely inappropriate pair of orange socks and brown shoes, and both of his meaty arms were locked around a bundle of canary-yellow life jackets. A navy sun hat covered his shiny bald head and made his pink ears fold over like tiny wings.

We all know it is wrong to judge someone simply by the way they look, but in this case I think we can make an exception. This man was very definitely weird.

He stopped suddenly beside a group of teenagers and threw the life jackets he had been carrying on to the sand. The teenagers were much too excited about going on a boat ride to notice all the odd things I've just described. Instead, the slippery giant stood very still and watched as

4

twelve teenagers playfully fought over the six life jackets. The winners were two boys and four girls, who would be the first to ride in the pea-green wooden fishing boat.

Accompanying the group was Daphne, an art teacher in her mid-forties. Daphne may have come from London, but she dressed just like the local women: hair pulled back in a loose knot, a swirling white cotton dress, a beaded necklace and a straw basket hanging over her shoulder. She had been to the Spanish town of Cadaqués on countless school art trips, but she had never before seen anyone like this big chap.

'What happened to the nice man who was here earlier?' asked Daphne, gesturing towards a small hut further along the beach. She had booked the boat ride with a handsome local man who had gone back to his hut to fetch the life jackets, and she'd been rather looking forward to seeing him again. Instead, she was now looking at one of the most unattractive human beings she had ever met.

The slippery giant replied too softly for Daphne to hear.

'I'm sorry, what did you say?' said Daphne. The man took a step towards Daphne and bent so that their faces were level. His mouth opened to speak and revealed a black tongue and lips, as if he had just been drinking a pot of ink. 'He's busy. I'm the skipper now,' was his reply. Daphne felt a shiver of goosebumps break out on her skin. For a moment she couldn't speak. It was all too strange and unexpected.

The man turned and waded into the water.

'Maybe we should wait until he comes back!' called Daphne, her voice rising with concern, but six of her students were already in the boat and the large man was climbing in with them, making it tip dramatically.

'No, stop!' shouted Daphne, and she ran towards the boat. But it was too late. The strange man had twisted the throttle and the water behind the motor was churned into foam. There was a scream. Shouting. But it wasn't any of her remaining students – they were still laughing and mucking about in the sand. The scream had come from somewhere else. Daphne turned and saw a crowd around the boatman's hut suddenly part and the handsome boatman appeared, clutching his nose.

'*Mi barco! Mi barco!*' cried the man as he stumbled towards Daphne, taking his hand away from his nose.

One of her students, a bubbly girl named Hannah Richards, screamed. The boatman's nose was bleeding and pointing entirely the wrong way.

'*Ese enorme hombre golpeó mi nariz y me robó el*

barco!' said the man with a great gasp, and Daphne felt her blood run cold.

'What did he say, miss?' wheezed Hannah.

'He said that huge man punched him on the nose and has stolen his boat,' said Daphne, her voice shaking, and she turned to look back out to sea. The little boat had already reached the rocky peninsula on the southern side of the bay. People were getting up from their beach towels and gathering around the bleeding boatman.

'I need a boat!' screamed Daphne. 'He's taken the children! We have to go after him!' Nobody responded because in her panic Daphne had forgotten to speak Spanish. '*Necesito un barco! Él ha robado a los niños!*' she pleaded, but her words were drowned out by the sound of an almighty explosion, so loud and powerful that everyone could feel it right down to their bones. Daphne looked out to sea. The little green fishing boat, the slippery giant and the six teenagers in her charge were gone! All that remained were thick swirls of blue smoke, twisting and drifting across the little port of Cadaqués.

LASAGNE

Exactly one week before that ghastly business with the explosion and the slippery giant, a spectacular dollop of lasagne sat steaming on a plate surrounded by buttered peas in the kitchen of a small terraced house in north-east London. The lasagne was about to be devoured by Nelson Green, an eleven-year old boy with shaggy brown hair, wide chocolate-brown eyes and a single brown freckle on the tip of his nose. Beside him sat the world's greatest big sister, sixteen-year-old Celeste. Curled around Nelson's feet was the oldest and smelliest mongrel of all time, Minty, who farted loudly but continued to snore like a donkey, and at the head of the table, wearing a dressing gown and with her wet hair wrapped in a towel, sat the scattiest woman in the entire universe, Nelson's mum. Between forkfuls of lasagne, Celeste carefully painted vivid green polish on to her mum's outstretched fingernails.

'That stuff smells too loud,' said Nelson disapprovingly.

'There's no such thing as a loud smell, Nelson,' chuckled Celeste. 'Mum, what time will you be home tonight?' Nelson tried to block the varnish vapours from getting up his nose by puckering his lips as if about to administer a big, slobbery kiss, but it was no use.

'It won't be a late one,' said Mum. 'Your father hates these company dinners more than I do.'

'What's it for?' Nelson's mouth was so full of lasagne it was hard to talk.

'Er, I think he said it had something to do with a conference he's got to go to in Brussels next week. Is that the place where the sprouts come from?'

She hadn't meant it as a joke but rather a genuine question. Nelson tried to stop himself laughing, but it backfired and sent lasagne shooting out of his nose instead.

'Nelson Green! That is disgusting!' barked his mum, recoiling in horror. 'And put your knees down! Why do you always have to crouch like a frog at the table?' Nelson corrected his posture, pulled a tissue out of his pocket and wiped his nose.

Celeste took hold of her mother's hands, gently pulled them towards her and soothingly said, 'You have to stay still, Mum, or it's gonna smudge.' As she resumed painting the nails, Celeste only needed to raise an eyebrow for Nelson to understand that he had better say sorry as soon as possible.

'Sorry, Mum,' said Nelson, and Celeste gave him a slow nod of approval as a receipt for following her telepathic orders. Nelson loved the way he and his sister could communicate without words. It was like having a secret code. They could have whole conversations just by nodding, glaring, raising their eyebrows or lowering their eyelids. Celeste and Nelson had never even discussed their code. They just knew what the other was thinking.

'Anyway, if their sprouts are anything to go by, I don't think I'd want go to Brussels much either,' said their mother.

Apart from Minty wheezing under the table, there was silence while Celeste resumed work on the last fingernail.

Nelson scooped up some peas, mashed them into the lasagne and then lifted a forkful to his mouth – delicious. He decided he could eat lasagne forever, and his stomach gurgled in agreement. 'All done,' chirruped Celeste as she screwed the cap back on to the bottle of varnish.

'You are a sweetheart,' said Mum, admiring Celeste's work.

'They look like witches' fingers,' mumbled Nelson, but his mum had heard him. There was a short pause before she decided now was the time to fire her 'secret weapon'.

'Oh, that reminds me, Nelson,' she said casually. 'I've put your name down for the school drama group.' With that bombshell, she rose from her chair.

Nelson was so appalled he dropped his cutlery with a loud clatter. Unfortunately, he had to struggle like mad to get any words past the enormous amount of lasagne currently occupying his mouth.

'Yes, I thought you'd like that,' Mum said with a wink to Celeste.

'What? Mum! Why would you do that?' begged Nelson.

'There, you see?' said his mother. 'You're really good at being dramatic.'

'No way. I don't wanna be in a play or act or any of that stuff!'

'Well, you've been at that school for nine months and you haven't made any friends yet. I mean, you don't even join in with sports any more.'

'That's cos my best friends went to Marchwood and I don't like anyone at St Patrick's,' pleaded Nelson.

It was true. He had had a few great friends at his primary school, but they had all gone on to the really expensive secondary school outside London and their promises to stay in touch and see each other at weekends had quickly evaporated.

'There's nothing wrong with St Patrick's. You're just a bit shy, and being in a drama group will force you out of that snail shell of yours.'

Nelson tried one last 'Please don't make me join

the drama club', and several really genuine-sounding versions of 'I hate that school!' but it was no use. His mother was already blowing her painted fingernails like a cowboy blowing his smoking guns after a particularly easy shoot-out.

Starting from Monday, Nelson would be joining the drama group. That was final. He looked at his lasagne and decided he'd had enough.

Celeste lay on her bed sending messages to her friends from her phone. Her mass of curly blonde hair radiated in all directions from her face like a child's painting of the sun. Whatever she was writing had made her smile – and Celeste had a big smile. She didn't just smile with her mouth, she smiled with her entire face. Add two rosy cheeks, a pair of shockingly blue eyes, a funny little gap between her two front teeth and you had the very definition of lovely. Like the sun, everyone enjoyed her presence, but more importantly, Celeste loved other people, especially her little brother, who was currently underneath her bed, angrily picking out fluff from her mattress. He'd done this since he was a baby, especially when he was feeling as annoyed as he did right now.

'Well, I'm not going to join that stupid drama group,' huffed Nelson, but he didn't get a reply.

The truth was, he *didn't* have any friends. There was always Simon Hopkins, but he was even shyer than Nelson. Sometimes Nelson would hang out at break with the Dempsey twins who were always glad of company, but Nelson didn't really like their games because they would take so long to set up the rules that break-time would be over before they had a chance to play anything.

The boy next door, Charles, had shown promise. But a few weeks back they had played swingball together and Nelson had accidentally hit the ball into Charles's face. Charles went silent, turned bright red, laid down his bat and climbed back over the wall to his own garden. Nelson didn't see him for at least a week, when he suddenly reappeared like a pigeon on the garden wall as if nothing had happened. Nelson found his constant presence on the wall a bit too weird and avoided going into the garden after that.

So that was that – Nelson was a loner. He knew it, his mum knew it and Celeste certainly knew it, but he didn't care. He'd got used to being on his own most of the time, and as long as he had Celeste he was just fine, thank you very much.

'Who are you sending messages to?' he asked.

'My friends,' said Celeste.

'It's all right for you. Everyone likes you. You're great at everything,' mumbled Nelson.

Celeste slid from her pillow and hung over the mattress to look directly at Nelson. Her hair spilled all over the carpet.

Nelson knew she was looking at him, but he was determined not to look back. 'Stop making that big face,' he said.

'I have told you the secret to making friends, young Jedi,' said Celeste in her best Yoda voice.

'You can't do Yoda. I do Yoda,' said Nelson dismissively, but that didn't stop Celeste.

'Start you must by pretending to be interested in other people. Only then will you discover, really interested in them you are. Do this and friends you will make.'

'Am I really late?' came the voice of Nelson's mum. Celeste sprang up out of Nelson's view to reveal his mother's stockinged feet hurriedly stepping into a pair of green high heels.

'The taxi has been outside for half an hour,' said Nelson.

'Oi. How's my little actor?' She crouched on the floor to peer at Nelson.

'Bye then,' said Nelson in his best bored voice, and his mother replied with a spectacular burp. Nelson couldn't help but chuckle.

'Gotcha,' said his mum, then rolled back on to her heels, kissed Celeste and clip-clopped along the landing and down the stairs.

'The keys are by the toaster,' shouted Celeste, but it was too late, the front door had closed. 'She's forgotten the keys again. I'm gonna have to stay up,' she said as Nelson wriggled from under the bed and looked out of the window to see his mother climbing into a taxi.

'Do you remember much about *your* mum?' asked Nelson.

He and Celeste only shared the same father. Celeste's mother had died when Celeste was just six years old. Apparently, their father's hair had turned white overnight and he didn't speak to a soul for almost three months. He would have stayed that way had it not been for the love and comfort of a scatty young lady, whom he eventually married. And that was the same lady who had just left in a taxi.

'I remember little things about her, like when she

stroked my hair my head would just fill up with really crazy dreams. I thought she was magic. And if I hurt myself or was sick or something, she'd tell me these amazing stories about her dad who found a jungle full of magical flowers.'

Nelson picked up a framed photo that sat by Celeste's

 bed. It was a picture that radiated happiness: a very chubby baby Celeste standing on a beach wearing a red polka-dot cap and matching swimming trunks. Her arms were raised above her head to hold on to the hands of her mother, who was bending over her and laughing so much you could almost hear it coming from the photograph.

'Sometimes I wonder if I'm like her. You know, what bits of me I get from her. Not magic fingers and stuff. I mean things like if I laugh or cry at the same things she would have done.'

Nelson put the photo down. 'If she was anything like you, Cel, your mum must have been brilliant.' Nelson breathed on the window and drew a smiley face in the condensation. Celeste pressed PLAY on her tiny iPod speaker system. The killer bassline of 'Seven Nation Army' by the White Stripes began to play, and just as he had done a million times before, Nelson marched around the bedroom like a soldier off to war.

'You'll be a great little actor, Nelson,' shouted Celeste.

'Silence, fool!' he commanded.

'I'm serious, you idiot! It'll be the best thing for you.'

'I'm gonna fight 'em off! A seven-nation army couldn't hold me back!' sang Nelson.

ADOLF HITLER IN A BOX

Celeste was right about almost everything, but not about the drama group. It was a huge mistake. Exactly one week later, Nelson was sitting backstage of the school theatre dressed in an oversized striped nightshirt with oven gloves on his hands. A small moustache and greased hair had given him the unmistakable appearance of Adolf Hitler – a clown version of Adolf Hitler. Never had he felt so miserable, nervous and humiliated all at once. He stared at his reflection in the mirror and considered his escape options.

A) Pretend to be too sick to go on stage. The trouble with this idea was that he'd left it too late to begin a believable decline in health.

B) Run for it. Not a great idea, as leaving the school at lunchtime would be considered an act of truancy and earn him a whole bunch of detentions. Also, looking like Hitler wearing oven

gloves while running down the street would be asking for trouble.
C) Just go through with it and never, ever come back to this stupid drama group ever again. Ever.

C was his only real option. He'd just have to stick it out. Anyway, the biggest problem was not the make-up or even the oven gloves, it was the play's writer, director and lead actor: Katy Newman.

Katy Newman blazed through her life with bulletproof confidence and truly believed that she was the boss of everything. It didn't bother her that no one else in her drama group was considered cool or even talented. All she needed were kids who would do exactly as she said without question. If they hadn't all followed Katy around like puppies they might have been friend material, but they did, so they weren't.

Katy's plays were notorious for handling serious subjects in an embarrassingly earnest style and they all involved Katy dying dramatically at the end. This lunchtime, St Patrick's school was to be subjected to *Alice in Nightmareland*, a spin on the traditional tale of Alice where the heroine was an evacuee whose fears were represented by scary life-sized versions of the toys she had brought with her on the train to the countryside. Nelson was playing Adolf Hitler as a jack-in-the-box. It was his job to pop out of the box and shoot Katy Newman with a starter pistol at the end of the play. Katy had fake blood ready to pour out of her chest. And if you think that's bad, then maybe now is a good time to tell you – this was also a musical.

'Twenty minutes before curtain-up, people. Last chance to use the loo,' sang Katy as she whizzed through the changing rooms. Katy was particularly excited today because a well-known casting director from London was visiting the school looking for 'cute and plucky kids' to be in a BBC drama set in the Second World War. In Katy's mind, this was probably the last play she would need to perform at the school. There was no doubt that once the casting director saw her in action it would be only a matter of days before she was on TV and more famous than the moon.

'If no one needs the loo, I think we should run lines once more just to be sure, OK?'

This made Nelson decide he should take Katy's advice and go to the toilet after all. He opened the door on to an empty corridor. The toilet was at the far end. He would have to make a run for it.

Nelson had never run anywhere so quickly. The fear of being spotted by someone while dressed as Adolf Hitler seemed to have infected his legs so that they now operated at gazelle-like speed. Had Mr Goff the sports teacher seen him in action, he would have insisted Nelson join the running team, but Nelson's impressive sprint was suddenly cut short as the toilet door he was aiming for swung open and three boys emerged. These were not just any boys; these were extremely cool Year 9s. Boys who could spit exactly the same way top football players do and who walked around school with the swagger of pirates. If they saw Nelson they would not only laugh their heads off until Nelson's face was redder than a pepper, he would almost certainly earn the nickname 'Nazi Nelson'. This was not a fate Nelson could bear, which is why his speedy legs changed course and he dashed through the first door on his left.

On the one hand, this had worked perfectly, and the cool Year 9 boys never caught a glimpse of him. However, Nelson was now standing in the middle of the girls' toilets, and the only thing worse than being seen by cool Year 9 boys would be being seen by cool girls. And the toilets were absolutely packed with them.

Nelson froze like a mouse who had accidentally run into a snake pit. He would never, ever be able to make friends after this. Who on earth would want to hang out with the Nazi who ran into the girls' toilets wearing oven gloves? He was about to go from zero to minus one hundred on the school popularity chart and winced at the prospect of how much his mother would laugh when she found out. He would have to change schools for sure now. Or, better still, move to the other side of the planet and start a new life on a nice remote island where the only inhabitants were coconuts. Nelson braced himself for an explosion of laughter. But it didn't happen. Instead, he opened his eyes to find that none of them were looking at him. They were all clamouring noisily to get a glimpse of Cheryl Corbett's tattoo (which Nelson later found out was actually a fake). Nelson inched slowly away from the girls and was just about to make his escape when the door flew open and smacked him right in the face. Nelson was slammed against the wall behind the door as five more girls ran into the toilet to see if the rumours about Cheryl's tattoo were true. He would have started to cry, but the need to remain unnoticed was so powerful it stemmed the flow of tears until he was well clear of the girls' toilets.

Phew.

Nelson snuck back through the door leading to the stage and decided it was safer to wait out the last few minutes before the show started inside his jack-in-the-box prop, which was waiting in the wings to be wheeled on with the rest of the scenery. It was small, dark and wonderfully quiet inside the box. He even had a cushion to sit on and a packet of Skittles left over from the last rehearsal. He also had a gun – the starter pistol Katy had borrowed without asking from the sports teacher's office.

It was halfway through his fourth Skittle and with only ten minutes to go before the play was due to start that it happened.

From inside the box, Nelson heard the stage door open and the unmistakable Welsh voice of his history teacher, Mr Mallison, speaking in urgent, hushed tones.

'There's no one in here, Judy. Now, tell me what's going on,' whispered Mr Mallison. Nelson could picture his hairy index finger pushing up the large square glasses that were forever trying to escape from his face by sliding down his long, thin nose.

Nelson didn't know who Judy was.

'Aw my gawd, I don't even know where to start,' said the woman, sounding hysterical.

Nelson was all ears. His eyes widened as though that might help him pick up a clearer signal.

'Just take a breath and start from the beginning, OK? What on earth has happened?' said Mr Mallison.

Nelson heard the woman sniff. The kind of big, snotty sniff you do after you've been crying for a while.

'I got a text. About ten minutes ago. It was from Daphne. There – there's been an accident. On the school trip to Cadaqués,' said the woman, her voice trembling. At this point Nelson felt as if all the air was sucked out of his lungs. Celeste was on that trip. She'd emailed him photos of her tour of the artist Salvador Dali's house. She was due back tomorrow. But he couldn't get distracted now – he had to listen.

'Happened about an hour ago. A bunch of the kids went on some kind of boat ride. There was an explosion.' The woman took another deep breath to steady herself.

Nelson pressed his ear against the side of the box.

'They found five of the kids floating out at sea,' she went on, her voice cracking.

'Oh my God – are they all right?' Mr Mallison was clearly horrified. The woman must have nodded, because Nelson heard Mr Mallison say, 'Oh, thank goodness for that.'

Nelson relaxed. Celeste was all right. This woman was just very upset. Phew.

'They had life jackets on apparently. But there'd been six kids in the boat, not five. One of them is missing.'

Nelson froze.

'Who? Who's missing, Judy?'

There was a pause. Nelson screwed his eyes up tight as

if he knew he was about to be hit by a truck-sized piece of information.

'Celeste Green.'

Nelson didn't move. He didn't breathe. He was just there. Frozen in time.

'Celeste? I don't believe it!' said Mr Mallison. 'How is this possible?'

'I don't know. Daphne texted me from the Spanish police station. You mustn't tell anyone yet, Bob. Her family have to be told first.'

You could hear the disbelief in Mr Mallison's reply. 'Celeste Green. Good Lord. Do they think . . . Judy, do they think she might be dead?' The conversation was cut short by the arrival of Katy and her team, setting up for the performance.

It wouldn't sink in. How could it? What Nelson had just heard was so enormously terrible, so gigantically awful, his brain could not even begin to make sense of it. The truth just sat there in front of him – a mountain – an ocean – a planet-sized fact he simply could not comprehend. No tears came to his eyes. He was too stunned to feel anything. Celeste. Dead. The two words just didn't connect.

Three and half minutes later Katy's awful play was in progress. The audience was only one-third full, mainly teachers, but you couldn't miss the casting director from London – a woman in her late fifties wearing a multicoloured shawl, cork high heels and gold hoop earrings. She was sitting in the front row and shifted awkwardly in her chair as if Katy's play was giving her stomach ache.

> *'Oh, is this a nightmare or is this a dream?*
> *Will I wake with a smile or wake with a scream?*
> *I miss my papa, and I miss my mumm-y.*
> *War is a nightmare for this poor evacuee.'*

Katy sang with such force and emotion that you could almost forgive her for not being in tune, but, I guarantee, if you had been in the audience you would only have been able to take this ghastly nonsense for a few minutes before you ran screaming for the exit.

The moment had come for Nelson to pop out of the box and sing a song about how he was going to invade England, before shooting Katy with the starter pistol. He knew the audience were waiting. He knew Katy was right on the other side of that box, but Nelson could not move a muscle. The news about his sister pressed down on him more heavily than a hat made of hippos.

Katy threw open the lid and glared at Nelson with enough hatred to boil a kettle. 'That's your cue. You're supposed to jump up and sing now,' she hissed, but Nelson was unable to move, let alone reply. Katy decided to take drastic action, grabbed Nelson by the armpit and lifted him up herself. The audience took one look at this befuddled little Adolf Hitler and started laughing out loud. 'Sing the song,' whispered Katy through gritted teeth, but all Nelson heard was a high-pitched ringing in his ears before his eyes fogged over and he suddenly fainted, tumbling forward, crushing the box, firing the starter pistol – BANG! – and sending Katy Newman toppling off the stage with a scream.

Mr Wheeler, the drama teacher, decided this might be a good time to close the curtain.

THE DAY THAT
FELL TO PIECES

The news that Adolf Hitler had shot Katy Newman in the middle of her play spread through the school on a wave of shocked whispers and giggles. Within ten minutes the story had been bent and twisted into even more colourful versions of the truth. This was precisely why Mr Mallison had waited until everyone, even the teachers, had returned to their classrooms, before leaving the backstage area with Nelson. Once the corridors were clear, Mr Mallison laid one of his large hands on Nelson's shoulders and they began a brisk walk to the headmistress's office.

It's funny how your body can get on without you at times. It doesn't need your approval for every heartbeat or reflex, and right now Nelson had never felt more detached from himself. He knew he was walking swiftly through the school; he could hear the footsteps from Mr Mallison's huge shoes echoing off the walls; he could see the corridors lined with paintings made by sixth-formers to illustrate climate-change issues; the anti-bullying posters and the photomontages of Year 7s planting vegetables in the new flower beds, but it felt as if his mind was separate from his body, like a kite on a long, long string floating high above it all. Connected, but only just.

Mr Mallison didn't knock; he just strode right into the secretary's office, making her jump up from behind her computer with a startled squeak.

'Sorry, Judy – I should've knocked but . . .' Instead of words, Mr Mallison finished his sentence with a nod of his head towards Nelson. Judy, a nervous, sparrow-like woman, nodded emphatically in reply, leaped to her feet and skittered across the room.

So this is Judy, thought Nelson. The woman he had heard breaking the news to Mr Mallison.

Judy knocked on the headmistress's door but didn't wait for a reply before opening it. The door swung open to reveal a large, wood-panelled room and the kind of desk Nelson had only ever seen presidents sitting behind in apocalyptic action movies. Mrs Vigars would have made a convincing world leader. A mighty oak tree of a woman wrapped in a dark blue dress and black cardigan with a burgundy scarf knotted around her neck. Her magnificent face was framed with dark hair pulled into a no-nonsense bun, and 'no-nonsense' was exactly the way in which she was speaking into her telephone right now.

'As soon as you hear anything more, you will call *me* first. No one else, do you understand, Daphne?' If I was Daphne, thought Nelson, I would totally understand, and even if I didn't, I would say I did. Mrs Vigars was seriously impressive and even put the phone down without saying goodbye. He'd seen her before in assembly, of course, but never up close. Wow.

*This is the portrait of Mrs Vigars that hung
in the entrance hall of the school.*

'Bob, couldn't you have at least cleaned him up a bit?' said the headmistress, rising from her chair and picking up a small black handbag, but she didn't wait for an apology. 'Your mother is going to be here very soon, Nelson, and I'm not sure she'll want to take you home looking like Hitler.' Mrs Vigars turned to her secretary with a cold, steely command. 'No calls, and get me some cotton pads.'

As Judy and Mr Mallison skittered away Mrs Vigars

opened her handbag and took out a packet of Werther's Original sweets and some baby wipes. She put a sweet in Nelson's hand and then popped one in her own mouth without taking her eyes off him. Nelson felt obliged to do the same. The sweet clacked around in his dry mouth like a pebble. Nelson could hear at least two telephones ringing in the secretary's office as Mrs Vigars led him to a seat by the window where a small mirror hung next to the most recent school photo. She handed Nelson the baby wipes, but Nelson just stood looking at them with no idea what to do.

'Never mind, I'll do it,' she said, and with one finger under his chin, Mrs Vigars tilted Nelson's face up towards her. She set to work. 'Eyes closed,' she said, and the cold wipes traced the lines of his face with soothing strokes. Mrs Vigars seemed to be paying particular attention to the place under his nose where the horrid little moustache had been painted.

'You're being very brave,' said Mrs Vigars.

'Have they found her yet?' Nelson whispered back.

'Not yet, but they will.'

'I don't think she's dead.'

'Neither do I.'

'Cel's a great swimmer. She probably swimmed away to a big rock or something.'

'Swam,' said Mrs Vigars, and Nelson could hear the smile in her voice. 'She probably *swam* away to a big rock.'

'Swam,' said Nelson. He heard the secretary enter the room as Mrs Vigars took the cotton pads from her and used them to apply a moisturizing cream.

'What's that?' asked Nelson.

'This is my special de-Hitler cream,' she said in mock seriousness. Nelson liked the smell of it. Coconut. The door creaked open once more and Nelson heard Mrs Vigars say, 'Ah, you must be Mrs Green.'

'Mum!' yelled Nelson, and turned towards the door, but instead of his mother, he was met by the sight of an extremely small woman who was as round and wrinkled as a turtle.

'No, no, no,' said the woman as she stepped forward. 'I'm a neighbour, aren't I, dear? Live three doors down. Hilda Mills.' Though in her late sixties, Hilda had thick curls of blonde hair and her glasses made it look as if she had joke-shop eyes.

'Where's Mum?' asked Nelson with real concern.

Unfortunately, Hilda was the kind of person who was incapable of answering a simple question with a simple answer.

'Oh, she's a mess. Well, she would be, wouldn't she? I mean, you hear about terrible things happening in foreign countries, but you never expect them to happen to you, do you? That's why I never go abroad. No. Just not safe, is it?'

'You're taking him home by car, I assume?' asked Mrs Vigars.

'Well, 'is mother can't drive, can she, not in the state she's in,' said Hilda in her rattling voice. 'Besides, she's busy packing.'

'Packing? For what?' asked Nelson, but Mrs Vigars stepped in.

'Mrs Mills, I appreciate you coming to collect Nelson. Now I think it's best if we let you get him home as quickly as possible.' The headmistress took one last look at Nelson's restored face and said, 'It's going to be all right.'

Nelson nodded. Mrs Vigars could have said she was from Mars and could melt cheese with her mind and he would have believed her. She was just one of those people you believed. And right now, believing that everything was going to be all right was a very good thing indeed.

Hilda parked her car in front of her own house and climbed out in a cloud of cigarette smoke before opening the door, which was protected with a childproof lock, for Nelson. 'I'll see you in, dear,' she said, and even though he really didn't want anything more to do with her, Nelson felt it best not to protest.

*

The first thing Nelson noticed was the two taxis parked outside his house. The drivers stood leaning against their cars, the apple-green front door was ajar, there were two open suitcases piled high with clothes by the door and Nelson could hear his mother's voice, thick with tears, coming from the kitchen. Inside, the house was a bomb site.

'Mum!' called out Nelson, and his mother came running towards him in her dressing gown, with the phone pressed to her ear and her face drenched with tears. 'He's here,' she sobbed into the phone, before falling to her knees and hugging Nelson as if she was trying to stop herself from falling down a hole. He'd seen his mother cry a million times – she would even cry at baby-wipe adverts ('Oh, it doesn't seem that long ago I was doing that for you!' she would gulp) – but he had never seen her so drained of happiness. It freaked Nelson out.

'Thanks for bringing me home, Hilda,' said Nelson, and made a move to close the door.

'I expect you want me to stay for a bit.'

'No, thanks.'

'Oh. Well, you know where I am if you need anything, dear,' were her last words before Nelson managed to close the door.

'Speak to your dad,' said his mother in a shuddering voice, and as Nelson took hold of the phone his mother crumpled on to the bottom step of the staircase.

'Dad?' said Nelson, and there was silence on the other end.

Then, 'Nelson, my love,' said his father, 'are you all right?'

Nelson nodded before remembering his father couldn't see him. 'Yes, Dad. I'm fine. Is there any news?'

Nelson's mum was trying to close one of the suitcases, but there was too much spilling from the sides for the locks to connect.

'They haven't found her yet, Nelson. But the police are looking, and we're going to help them.'

'There are two taxis outside, Dad.'

'Yes. Listen, Nelson, I'm going to fly straight to Spain from Brussels, OK? Your mother is meeting me in Cadaqués, and I need you to get her into one taxi. Her plane leaves in two hours.'

'What about me?'

'Nelson, I need you to be really grown up now. You are going to take the other taxi and go and stay with Uncle Pogo. Remember him?'

'No!' pleaded Nelson. 'I'm coming with you!'

'Nelson, I know this is horrible, but we don't know what to expect and we can't take you with us.'

'I'm not staying with Uncle Pogo. He's a nutcase.'

'I promise you, we'll be back before you know it, and everything is going to be fine.' Nelson felt his father wasn't telling the truth.

'Who's going to look after Minty?' he said, spying the

dog fast asleep by the back door.

'Hilda's agreed to pop in and feed him.'

'I could stay here too then.'

'Look, we have to do this, and you just . . . you just have to be my big guy, all right? Get your mother in that taxi, Nelson – she cannot miss that plane. OK?'

'OK,' said Nelson.

'I have to go now, Nelson.'

'OK. Bye.'

Nelson put the phone back on its base and noticed the flashing red message light. There were twelve new messages. They'd never had that many messages before.

Every single thing about today was crazy.

In less than two minutes Nelson had gathered some clothes for his mother to wear, fetched her wallet and passport from his father's desk drawer and closed both her cases. One of the drivers took the luggage and Nelson's mother dropped into the back seat of his taxi before lurching forward to kiss Nelson.

'Did your play go all right, love?' she mumbled.

'Yeah, fine.' Nelson looked at the taxi driver. 'She mustn't be late.' The driver nodded and started the engine. Nelson kissed his mother, closed the door and the taxi drove away.

'So I'm taking you to Hammersmith – Box Elder Drive, is that right?' said the second taxi driver.

'Er, yeah,' said Nelson. 'I'll just go and get my bag.'

UNCLE POGO

Uncle Pogo's house had to be the most badly kept home in the whole of England. The front garden was piled high with bizarre artefacts gathered from boot sales and skips which made it seem less like a home, more like a graveyard for weird stuff and it would be hard to imagine a more unwelcoming entrance than the corrugated steel front door sprayed with the words: BEWARE DOG.

Nelson's heart sank even lower than it had been before. He paid the driver and dragged his rucksack out of the taxi, triggering the security light above Uncle Pogo's front gate. The monstrous garden was instantly flooded with the kind of blinding light you would expect from a spaceship trying to beam you up, and a dog inside the house began barking like crazy. Though Nelson

couldn't see the dog, he could tell that this was the bark of an animal that would enjoy chewing your shoes to shreds, preferably while you were still wearing them.

Nelson shielded his eyes from the light as he hauled his bulging rucksack on to his back. He hadn't wanted to think about how long he would be away, so he had just taken everything from his drawers and stuffed it in.

Behind him he could hear the rattle of the taxi which was lingering while the driver argued on the phone with his wife over their holiday plans.

Still dazzled by the security light, Nelson groped around for the bell, but all he felt was cold rusty metal and the alarming thud of the crazed dog leaping repeatedly against the other side of the door. The security light suddenly switched off, and as Nelson's eyes slowly adjusted to the gloom he spotted a piece of paper that was stuck to the door with thick silver tape.

Nelson reached for the note and then spun around to see the taxi driver pulling away. 'Stop! Wait!' he yelled, waving his one free arm over his head. 'I have to go to St Paul's Cathedral.'

Hello Nelson

Come at once to the exact address written on the back. Hopefully the taxi is still there to take you. I will explain all when you get here.

Be quick

Uncle Pogo

38

As the taxi rocketed along the Victoria Embankment, narrowly missing a cyclist here and there, Nelson sat frozen, wondering why his parents could ever have thought staying with Uncle Pogo was a safe option.

He watched bits of London flash by. The Millennium Wheel, Waterloo Bridge, the great Lego blocks of the South Bank . . . all looked reassuringly solid against the gathering rain clouds and the great unknown he was zooming towards. He zipped his jacket a little higher and felt something hard in the top pocket, like a frozen pea pressed against his chest and his brain was suddenly flooded with a memory.

The pendant.

He had Celeste's pendant in his pocket. He had been carrying it since the day she left for Spain. She'd been so excited about going but when he'd said goodbye to her she'd known he was sad to see her go. 'Wear this,' she had said, and taken off her pendant.

'I'm not wearing a girl's necklace,' Nelson had snorted.

'This isn't just any old necklace. It's my lucky charm. It belonged to my mum. And it's magic.'

'Yeah, right,' Nelson had said sarcastically.

'You won't ever be sad with this on,' said Celeste, and she'd hung it around his neck. Once she was out of sight,

Nelson had taken it off. A cloudy red stone, no bigger than a pea, clasped by little silver leaves on the end of a silver chain as thin and as delicate as spider's silk. How could anything this unremarkable be magic? He had forgotten all about it and now, suddenly, everything made sense.

The necklace. Celeste's lucky charm. She wasn't wearing it in Spain and that's why something terrible had happened to her. The great big impossible truth he had not been able to swallow suddenly dropped into his stomach like a bowling ball. Celeste, the most wonderful big sister of all time, was gone, maybe even dead. *Dead.* That thought suddenly packed such a punch that it knocked all the air from Nelson's lungs. He started to cry. He must have had a hidden reservoir in his head just for tears because they poured like his head had sprung two leaks all the way to his destination.

The taxi pulled off the main road and hurtled down increasingly narrow roads. Nelson braced himself, one hand against the window, the other gripping the pendant.

There was a sudden screech of brakes, and Nelson slid off his seat on to the well-padded backpack.

'St Paul's!' the taxi driver barked through the intercom, and Nelson climbed out, relieved to be in one piece and free from the death wish of his driver.

The storm clouds began rumbling overhead and as the taxi drove off it seemed to Nelson as if he was the only living thing around. No cars, people or even pigeons. Just the sound of a police siren wailing in the distance. It was as if everyone knew there was a massive storm coming and only someone really stupid would be standing in the street without an umbrella right now. Nelson buried his nose in the crook of his arm and let his coat soak up the tears left in his eyes.

So much for the lucky pendant.

If it really was magic and brought you good luck, then there was no way Nelson would be standing all on his own on the streets of London with the promise of being drenched by a storm at any second. Even so, Nelson put the necklace on and tucked the stone under his T-shirt.

This is St Paul's Cathedral.
If you look carefully, you can see a man up there.

'Nelson!' called a voice but there was no one to be seen. The doors to St Paul's were shut and the pizza restaurant opposite looked empty.

'Nelson! Ahoy!' cried the voice again. Nelson looked up at the magnificent dome of the cathedral to see a tiny figure dressed in an orange boiler suit clinging to a rope.

'You got my note then!'

And with that, the little orange figure began abseiling down the side of the building towards a van with the words POGO PLUMBING written on the side. Nelson blinked. You don't expect to see a plumber dangling off the side of a cathedral.

'Won't be a mo!' said the man, and precisely one mo later he seemed to lose control of the ropes and made a sudden dash to earth. There was a yelp followed by a SNAP! as he fell from the rope and dropped into a chubby little bush far below.

Nelson ran, dragging his stupidly big backpack with him. He half expected to find a mangled man impaled on a branch.

'Uncle Pogo! Are you all right?'

'Uh, y-yes. Yep. Ooof. Think so. Might have twisted my, er . . .' said the orange man as he plopped out on to the grass.

42

Uncle Pogo got to his feet and brushed the leaves and twigs from his overalls and hair. He was a strange sight – well over six feet tall and thin all over except for his belly, which looked as if he had stuffed a cushion up his jumper. Short curly orange hair clung to the top of his head, matching the lurid colour of his overalls, his pale skin was peppered with freckles and his cheeks were set in a permanent blush of red. But the most striking thing about him was his right foot: it was pointing backwards. If you had twisted your leg like this you would be in agony, but where you or I have a knee and a shin with a foot on the end of it, Uncle Pogo had a plastic leg. 'Just a tick,' he said, before leaning all his weight on to the right leg and turning his entire body around it. It made a grinding sound, just like a pepper mill, followed by a click as the foot was reset.

Nelson found it hard to believe that his parents had thought this was a good idea. 'Hello, Uncle Pogo,' he said.

'Crikey O'Mikey, you were only this big when I last saw you,' said Uncle Pogo, one hand suggesting the same height as his hips. 'Maybe you'll turn out to be a big'un like me, eh?' and he hopped back towards his van.

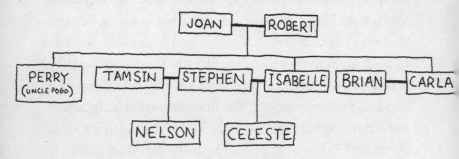

You might need to refer to this family tree a little later on in the story, so make a note of this page number.

As you can see, Uncle Pogo was actually called Perry and he was the big brother to twin sisters Carla and Isabelle (Celeste's mother). This meant he wasn't actually related to Nelson at all, but the whole family had always called him Uncle Pogo – it just seemed to fit. The name Pogo had been bestowed upon him when he arrived at primary school because of his initials: Perry Oliver Graham Osborne, Pogo for short. Pogo grew up wanting to be a rugby player, but that all ended the night of a terrible tragedy. His sisters had been caught in a fire at their family home and while he was trying to rescue them a wall had fallen and crushed his leg.

His rugby days were over, but being an eccentric and

inventive soul, he had fashioned himself a new leg out of
fibreglass and decorated it with orange and white stripes
like a traffic cone.

According to Celeste,
Pogo's leg had hidden
compartments and the
kind of gizmos you would
expect from a Swiss Army
knife. (Nelson had never
seen any sign of this being
true.) Pogo found a new
career as a plumber
and general fix-it man.
Being both reliable
and extremely able, he
was never out of work.
However, none of this explained
what he'd been doing on the top of St Paul's Cathedral.

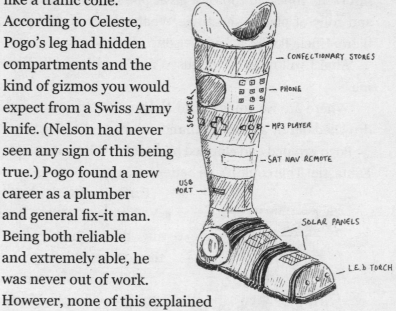

The back doors of the van had also been painted with the
POGO PLUMBERS logo (the letters in the style of pipes),
but someone had scratched out
the 'G', so that now it read PO O
PLUMBERS. Normally Nelson
would have found this kind of
thing hysterical, but right now
he was feeling far from normal.
He was confused, tired and,

if he was honest, pretty scared, but Uncle Pogo was too busy to notice. He opened the rear doors of his van and threw his ropes on top of a great pile of pipes and rolls and rolls of plastic sheeting. 'What were you doing up there, Uncle Pogo?' asked Nelson.

'Aha! I will reveal all in just a mo,' said Pogo. 'Follow me.'

'Where are we going?' said Nelson, but his voice was drowned out by a massive thunderclap.

Pogo grinned and clapped his hands. 'Whoa, it's close. Fantastic! This couldn't be better timing.'

'Timing for what?' asked Nelson. 'What are you doing here?' The thunder rumbled again.

'I'll show you where you'll be sleeping first.' Uncle Pogo picked up his bag of tools and headed towards the front of the cathedral.

It was at this point that it started to rain. Not a gentle pitter-patter but a sudden crash of water being flung down from the thunderous sky,

46

chasing Nelson and Uncle Pogo up the steps of St Paul's.

'Well, this should be a cosy place to spend the night,' joked Nelson as they reached the grand entrance.

'I'm very glad you think so,' said Pogo.

'I was joking, Uncle Pogo. We're not actually sleeping in here, are we?'

'No, no,' he chuckled, 'you can't go sleeping on the floor of St Paul's Cathedral.'

Nelson breathed a great sigh of relief.

'We'll be sleeping downstairs, in the crypt,' said Uncle Pogo. 'Follow me.'

ONE DEAD NELSON

St Paul's Cathedral can seat at least two thousand people, so right now Nelson felt as if he and Uncle Pogo were alone inside the dark and vast belly of a whale. If this had been a normal visit, Nelson would have been gazing up at the incredible arches and marvelling at the sheer scale of the dome, but at night, with the only light coming from a few emergency exit lights, it was all far too creepy for him.

'Look at this poor fellow,' said Pogo as they reached a very large marble statue wrapped in plastic sheets. The storm must have been directly overhead by now, because there was hardly a gap between each roar of thunder and shock of lightning that briefly illuminated the impressive figure of a man riding a horse.

'There's a leak, and the water is completely ruining his lovely looks. Our mission is to find the leak and save the statue!' Pogo grinned, but his excitement wasn't quite rubbing off on Nelson. 'Follow me,' said Uncle Pogo, before limping towards a stone staircase on their right. 'It's like a great big colander. The dome, I mean. Holes everywhere. In fact, you could say this is a very *holy* place! Ha ha! Do you get it? *Holy*! Ha ha ha! Anyway, this place has leaks galore, and every time it rains it's causing more and more damage, not to mention playing havoc with the electrics. Shot to bits from what I gather. They patched up all the holes they could find, but somehow the water's still . . . You look confused – are you all right?'

'No, I get it,' Nelson replied, but in truth he hadn't taken in a word his uncle said.

'Anyway, they've tried all sorts to fix it,' said Uncle Pogo, his voice echoing off the walls as they descended the dark staircase. 'Even had teams of specialists from those wonderful cathedrals in Venice. But none of it worked. I know one of the priests here – used to play rugby together – and he put me up for the job of solving the problem once and for all. So here we are. Welcome to base camp, Nelson.' Uncle Pogo unhooked a torch hanging from his utility belt and pointed it into the darkness. The beam of light illuminated a circle of bone-coloured pillars surrounding two tents; one large and brown, the other small and orange. Between these was a large black tomb that rose high from a stone plinth on an intricately patterned tiled floor. With a shock that almost stopped his heart, Nelson saw his own name written on the side of the tomb.

It was worse than any nightmare he had ever had. Imagine seeing your own grave!

'Ta-da! You'll be sleeping right next to the one and only Admiral Nelson. The two Nelsons! You can keep each other company.' On closer inspection Nelson saw the full name of the man inside the black tomb.

HORATIO · VISC · NELSON

Admiral Nelson. The same man who stands proudly on a column with pigeons on his head in Trafalgar Square. He may have been a noble and famous leader, but all Nelson could think about now was that he was going to be sleeping in a big scary room next to a dead guy. 'You're probably hungry, eh? Growing lad and all that. Of course you are. Why don't you grab something to eat while I finish setting up? I put a lunch box in your tent.' Uncle Pogo busied himself lighting paraffin lamps and placing one at the base of each column.

In the gloom of the tent Nelson could see a pile of grey blankets and a pillow stacked at the far end. His inflatable mattress was clearly made for use in a swimming pool, as it had dolphins printed all over it and a hole on each side for your drink. Nelson pulled his backpack in after him, nearly bringing the entire tent down when it rolled backwards against the side.

Next to the pillows and blankets he found a shoe box with the words FOOD FOR NELSON written on the lid in felt-tip. He realized that he really was hungry and opened the box to find two more boxes: AM and PM.

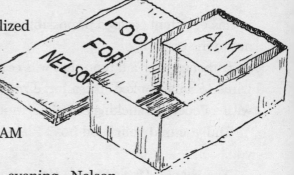

As it was the evening, Nelson opened the box marked PM and found three smaller labelled boxes. Inside STARTER he found a Peperami bent double to fit in. He didn't fancy a spicy sausage right this minute, so he opened the next box. Inside MAIN COURSE was a Scotch egg (a Scotch egg is a hard-boiled egg under a layer of sausage meat and the whole thing's covered in breadcrumbs). This Scotch egg bore the smell of something very wrong indeed. Nelson almost didn't dare open the last box. But he *was* hungry. How bad could it be? When he slid open the box marked PUDDING he found a teaspoon and a large wad of tin foil. He peeled the foil back to reveal what he thought at first to be maggots but then recognized as rice pudding. Nelson loved rice pudding, but this gloopy mess, and the smell of the Scotch egg, had completely short-circuited his pangs of hunger. The idea of sleeping on a pool lilo in this eggy tent seemed impossible, so he ventured back out to the crypt.

Hunched over a laptop that was connected by several wires to what looked like a large radio, Uncle Pogo sat with a Peperami sticking out of his mouth like a cigar.

'Did you find your food box? I labelled everything for you.'

'Yes, thanks, Uncle Pogo,' said Nelson, still trying hard not to retch from the smell of rotten egg.

'Look at this. A 3D model of the entire cathedral,' said Pogo proudly, his eyes fixed on the screen which was lit by a rotating outline of the building. 'All the red dots are barium sensors. You know what barium is?'

Nelson shook his head.

'Oh, it's a very handy chemical. I've covered the whole roof in it. That's what I was doing when you arrived. So now, when the rain leaks into the building, it will carry the barium with it, and these clever little sensors will lead me straight to the—' Pogo was interrupted by a loud alarm. The screen flashed and one of the sensors lit up.

'There she blows! Level 1. Ha ha! Nelson, the time has come to save the day!' Like a cheesy special effect, the entire crypt exploded to a flash of lightning accompanied by a knee-knockingly loud roll of thunder.

'Let's suit up,' said Uncle Pogo, and before Nelson had time to ask why, he and his uncle were wearing rubber boots, head-to-toe waterproof ponchos and balaclavas

with torches strapped to either side of their heads right
where their ears were hiding.

This is what they looked like.

'Ready?' asked Pogo with a big grin.

'I don't want to do this, Uncle Pogo,' said Nelson,
which, when you think about it, seems fair enough.

'Oh.' Uncle Pogo seemed to be noticing his nephew's
lack of enthusiasm for the first time. Nelson had only
just begun to come to terms with the idea that Celeste
was missing and now he was dressed up like a loony and

about to go looking for leaks in St Paul's Cathedral. He just wanted something to make sense. To be normal. And he certainly didn't want to cry in front of his uncle.

Pogo awkwardly reached out and grabbed Nelson's shoulder. It was meant as a reassuring gesture, but Uncle Pogo was not familiar with being supportive and ended up nearly knocking Nelson over.

'Sorry.' He shuffled awkwardly. 'Erm, look, they'll find Celeste, Nelson. I'm absolutely sure they will.'

'I just wanna go home,' mumbled Nelson as he looked down at his rubber boots.

'Yes, well, sitting around brooding will only make you feel worse. But I know what the solution is.'

'What?'

'Keep busy and keep moving,' said Pogo. 'Oh, and music!' He reached down to his fake right leg and pressed a switch just below his knee. Music began to boom from his shin. 'Oh ho! That's more like it!' Nelson was amazed. His uncle's leg had a built-in speaker from which 'You Can Call Me Al' by Paul Simon was now blasting around the cathedral loud enough to rattle Admiral Nelson's bones. Pogo grabbed hold of the torches on either side of Nelson's head and switched them on. 'OK, Nelson Green. We have music, lights and now it's time for action!' Nelson was swept up in Uncle Pogo's madness. The musical leg was undeniably bonkers and if Uncle Pogo's plan was to keep Nelson's mind off his sister, he had just succeeded.

THE SECRET LABORATORY

ENGLAND EXPECTS EVERY MAN TO DO HIS DUTY

These were the words written in mosaic tiles on the stone at the foot of the second flight of steps they were about to climb. 'The words of Admiral Nelson,' said Uncle Pogo, pointing and talking loudly over Paul Simon. 'And it is our duty to find and repair this leak!' As they stomped up the stairs, Nelson could hear his uncle's laptop beeping faster. He had seen enough action movies to know this meant they were getting closer to the target (although if this was a movie the target would be something more exciting than a leak, and they certainly wouldn't be dressed up like *this*).

The rubber boots Nelson had been forced to wear were way too big for him and made the climb an exhausting experience. When they reached the top Pogo pulled out his laptop and flipped open the screen. An image of St Paul's appeared covered in little red dots. One of the red dots was flashing, and when Pogo hit the return button, the image zoomed in on it. 'We should find the leak right around . . .' He scanned in closer to the flashing dot and a huge smile came to his face. 'Ah, we've come up too high. Idiot. Must be down there.'

He switched off the music and there was a delicious silence.

'Sorry about that, Paul Simon, but we will need to use our ears now. Follow me, Nelson.' Nelson kept up with his uncle as best he could as he hurried back towards the stairs. At the bottom there was a long corridor lined with prints of the cathedral in various states of construction down one side and great stone arches down the other.

'These are the buttresses. They hold everything up. Superb design.' Pogo was gazing up at the ceiling admiringly. 'And through here we should find . . .' He wrestled with a key in a lock and opened a door into a magnificent library. Nelson's torches revealed the eerie stone busts of men wearing large wigs and proud expressions on their faces.

He turned around and realized he had walked to the opposite side of the library to his uncle, who was pressing his ear against a gap between two bookcases. 'Here! Listen!' said Uncle Pogo with such delight that Nelson found himself running towards him.

Uncle Pogo was right. Nelson could hear rushing water on the other side of the wall. 'Maybe there used to be a door or maybe . . .' Uncle Pogo pulled off his rubber gloves and pressed his hands against the wall. Crouching low, he took one hand away. With a smile as wide as his

This is the library at night.
It's very dark in here, which is why you
can't see very much.

entire head, Uncle Pogo showed Nelson that his hand was covered in white, wet plaster.

Using a crowbar from his toolbox, Uncle Pogo managed to create a split in the wall that ran vertically from just above his head down to the floor. There was a loud CRACK as the split reached the floor, immediately followed by water rushing out of the bottom and a smell that was so bad it would make your nose want to quit its job for good.

'Stand back,' cried Uncle Pogo, and grabbing the open seam with both hands he pulled as hard as he could. More water gushed across the floor. Filthy, stinking water. Something bumped against his ankle, and when Nelson looked down his headlamps lit up several dead rats. His instant reaction was to jump back, but all this did was splash the horrible smelly water all over his jeans.

'That's as far as it will go for now, but I wonder if . . .' Uncle Pogo peered into the gap he'd made. 'I can see it!' He picked up his toolbox and tried to wedge his entire body into the gap he had made. No chance.

'Nelson, over here.'

'It really stinks,' protested Nelson, sloshing through the water, whose flow was now subsiding.

'A smell won't do you any harm. Now look. Do you see it? At the back, up high.'

Nelson peered through the gap and his headlamps illuminated a windowless chamber about the size of his headmistress's office. There was an iron chandelier hanging from the ceiling, which would have once held candles and against the far wall there were two stone sinks without taps. Above them a large pipe that ran the length of the room had snapped through and the end that hung loose was spewing water all over the floor.

'Here,' said Uncle Pogo, handing Nelson the toolbox. 'It'll be dead easy. I'll talk you through it.'

'What? I'm not going in there,' protested Nelson, his voice suddenly higher-pitched than usual.

'Oh, you'll be fine. It's a piece o' cake. And it's only to stop the water for now. I'll need some back-up in the morning to get this to open wider before I can repair it properly,' said Uncle Pogo. Nelson just stood there. 'Please,' said Uncle Pogo, with a sorry look on his face. 'It'll only take a minute. Then we can go home.'

He really did want to go home, so Nelson took a deep breath and, holding his nose, squeezed through the gap. Once he was on the other side, Uncle Pogo handed him the toolbox and a large roll of silver industrial-strength sticky tape. Nelson turned around and focused his headlamps on the broken pipe. The rest of the room was way too creepy and he certainly didn't want to look into the dark corners.

'Now you just need to find something to stand on so you can reach the pipe,' said Uncle Pogo, his face squished into the gap.

Nelson was forced to look around, and the lamps on his ears revealed an eerie sight. The room stretched back further than he had thought and ended at a large black wooden door. One side of the room was lined with furniture-sized objects covered by filthy torn sheets, like a group of oddly shaped people in bad ghost costumes.

'Can you see anything to stand on, Nelson?' asked Uncle Pogo.

Nelson selected the tallest thing he could see: a narrow table under a particularly mouldy sheet. 'There's a table, Uncle Pogo. I'll try and move it.'

He took a few steps through the filthy water towards the table, grabbed the edge and pulled. There was a horrid scraping nose as the metal legs ground against the stone floor.

'That's it, Nelson. Now put the toolbox on the table, and once you're up there I'll talk you through what you need to do.'

Nelson tried to climb on without disturbing the horrible sheet.

'The pipe will likely be made of lead, so it'll be easy to bash it back into place with the mallet – not the hammer,' called Uncle Pogo. 'But have the tape around your wrist so you can tear off a strip and wrap it around as quickly as possible.'

The table gave a shake, which made Nelson gasp. 'It's quite wobbly, Uncle Pogo.'

'I'm not surprised. It's probably hundreds of years old! Now you want to get the two ends of the broken pipe to meet, or at least as close together as possible. So you're gonna whack that loose end with the mallet until it's back where it should be. Got it?'

Nelson gave his uncle a thumbs-up, lifted the mallet out of the toolbox and looked up at the offending pipe. The stench was awful, and his body made all the movements necessary to be sick without actually being sick.

Just get it done and get out, thought Nelson, and he swung the mallet at the hanging pipe. The pipe *was* made of lead and it bent back into position after only a few blows.

'Yessss!' cried Uncle Pogo as if Nelson had just scored a goal in the World Cup. 'Now tape it up with a few short pieces first.'

The two ends of the broken pipe were now only couple of centimetres apart but the vile water was hissing out right into Nelson's face.

Nelson spat to get the water out of his mouth and tore a length of tape from the roll.

Just as he was reaching up to tape it closed, the entire pipe dropped back down and shot him with a face full of water. Off balance, Nelson fell and landed flat on his back on the table. If this had been a normal table he would have sat straight back up, but what Nelson and Uncle Pogo didn't know was that, hidden under the sheet, the table was covered in hundreds of tiny metal spikes which pierced Nelson's poncho and stuck right into his skin.

'Nelson! You all right?' shouted Uncle Pogo. But Nelson just lay there, not moving or making a sound.

'Oh no. Oh no. Oh no,' panted Uncle Pogo, in complete panic. From Uncle Pogo's point of view, Nelson was in a very bad way, but from Nelson's point of view things could not be better.

You would have thought that landing on a bed of spikes would be extremely painful, but all Nelson felt right now was bliss. In fact, it felt as if his body was melting like butter in a frying pan. The terrible smell in the room had left his nostrils and his nose was filled with the scent of the rose soap they kept in the downstairs toilet at home. As his eyes closed he was looking up at trees, and sunshine was peeping through the green leaves. It was clear to Nelson where he was now – in his back garden on a perfect summer's afternoon. A memory brought back to life so completely that he was reliving it with every part of his body. He was sitting on a stool and Celeste was cutting his hair. Celeste wasn't missing at all. She was right there, standing in the garden with a comb clenched between her teeth and a pair of scissors snipping away at his fringe. Charles from next door sat on the garden wall watching them like a pigeon. Celeste's hands smelled of the rose soap. She leaned forward. 'Close your eyes,' she said, and for a moment all Nelson could feel was his sister blowing the hair off his face. When he opened his eyes again, he was looking straight at her pendant. The pendant she always wore. The pendant that was supposed to bring good luck. The pendant she had given to him when she left—

And all at once the dream ended and Nelson screamed the most terrible scream.

Uncle Pogo was tearing at the wall and trying to squeeze his body through the gap. 'Nelson! Nelson! Get up!' he cried, but Nelson could not move. Even his breathing had stopped and he could hear a high-pitched whistle, like several kettles reaching boiling point. Nelson didn't know this, but the sound was coming from beneath the table, where there were seven copper test tubes held in a row by an iron rod. The copper had turned green after hundreds of years of neglect and each test tube fizzed and steamed and spat as if someone was pouring invisible hot fat into them. The whistling, screaming sound got louder and louder as the test tubes shook and sputtered and the whole table rattled as if it was furious. It was like an end-of-the-world-style earthquake and everything was screaming and there was steam and heat and pain and . . .

It was over. Completely over, as if it had never happened. Nelson sat bolt upright and gasped as if he had been holding his breath all this time.

'Nelson!' cried Uncle Pogo.

Nelson rolled off the table and stood on shaky legs. 'I'm OK,' he mumbled, and with that he passed out and fell to the floor with an almighty splash.

Luckily Nelson had fallen close enough to the gap in the wall for Uncle Pogo to reach with his right arm and drag him through. The next time his eyes opened he was lying on his back in the orange tent and being tucked under blankets. Uncle Pogo was looking down at him with real concern.

'I'm totally OK,' said Nelson weakly.

'I'm such an idiot. I should never have asked you to do that. I'm so sorry. I'd take you home, but I think you're better off resting up here for a bit. You won't tell your folks about this, will you?' said Uncle Pogo, half joking but with a hint of real desperation.

Nelson nodded. And smiled. Once again he felt all his sadness and worry and fear leave his body, as if he was sinking back into that happy feeling, like a great warm bath.

'I feel great, just tired . . .' He yawned and another

dream, this time of eating lasagne, Minty at his feet, washed over him.

The storm had passed. The sky was black and the puddles were great inky mirrors reflecting the orange lamplight. Uncle Pogo had already been on the phone to the caretakers and his contact at the Museum of London, who were coming as quickly as they could. Pogo was well aware that not only had he found the source of the leak, he had also stumbled across something special. A hidden chamber. This was bound to be of interest, even if it was rather smelly and gloomy-looking.

As Pogo gathered the tools he would need to repair the lead pipes, something truly extraordinary was happening above . . .

Back in the filthy hidden chamber, beneath the bed of nails, the seven green copper vials appeared to be trembling in their metal stand. When Nelson fell on the table he had switched on a machine that had lain dormant for hundreds of years, and now, like eggs about to hatch, these vials contained something that was alive and growing. Something that wanted to get out. And each one was making a very distinct noise. Awful gurgling noises came from one of the tubes. From another, a sound like popcorn being made. The strange chorus of hissing and belching and growling and moaning reached such a crescendo that the test tubes began to topple and fall

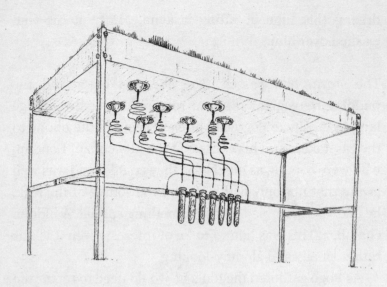

from the iron holder. The contents of each vial floated out into the filthy water on the chamber floor, like disgusting croutons in a horrible soup.

The strangest things you've ever seen. A tiny eyeball, alive, blinking and swelling in size. A tongue rolling and stretching like a slug in salt, a bird-sized claw flexing and scraping against the stone, a tentacle like those of an octopus, which wrapped itself around a squashy green ball but quickly let go when the ball erupted in spikes like a cactus. A scarlet, crescent-shaped object began to peel itself like a banana, to reveal a black horn underneath, while a little purple sponge blossomed with thick fur and released a cloud of purple ink into the water. Though these strange and ugly and noisy little things looked and behaved completely differently from each other, they all had one thing in common: they were growing very, very quickly indeed.

PROFESSOR DOODY AND THE VANISHING TOAST

Nelson's eyes snapped open. Something was moving outside his tent. A hurried sort of shuffling against the stone floor. It wasn't the shuffling that alarmed Nelson; it was the fact that it had stopped so suddenly and he had heard a faint but urgent whisper. It was silent again. Worryingly silent. Nelson blinked quickly, his eyelids the only part of him that was awake right now. His body was way behind. He felt as if he had been dropped from a great height and landed with a splat on the airbed.

There it was again. Shuffling, this time even closer to his tent. The paraffin lamps threw just enough light on to his tent to cast shadows of the pillars, but some of those shadows were on the move. Odd little shapes moving too quickly to be identified. Nelson took a deep breath and was about to call out when his tent suddenly shook and a snake-like shape slithered across the top of it. Nelson's eyes widened in fear. If this was a snake, it was long enough to be the kind that could eat a man whole and heavy enough to make the top of the tent bulge down towards Nelson's face. The end of 'the thing' whipped against the top of the tent as it dropped

68

to the crypt floor with a thud.

'Get up,' Nelson urged his body, but his body was having none of it. There it was again. Frantic indiscernible whispers, shuffling feet and the scrape of something large snaking its way all around Nelson's tent. Fear made his heart pound faster. Nelson wanted to call out to his uncle, but all he managed to utter was the first syllable: 'Unk!' Big mistake. Whatever had been slithering and whispering clearly heard and it stopped. For a moment there was complete silence. Then the tent twitched, and from the corner of his left eye Nelson could see the entrance zip starting to move. Now he really wished he hadn't called out. Whatever the thing was, it knew he was here and it wanted to get inside the tent! The zip rose slowly at first and then stopped abruptly. There was a low growl and the tent shook so violently that Nelson thought his heart might explode with fear. The growling became louder and louder as the tent shook and shook and shook and suddenly the tent burst open.

'Graaaaaar – Ruddy zip!' said the enormous face of Uncle Pogo, leaning in through the tent flaps. Nelson felt his fear burst like a dam and he was suddenly flooded with relief. The log-mode his body had been in instantly lifted and he was able to roll on to his back. 'Didn't wake you up, did I?' said Uncle Pogo.

'I thought it was . . .' croaked Nelson, but he decided not to finish his sentence. The idea of giant snakes and strange creatures had quickly switched from terrifyingly real to utterly ridiculous.

'I'm just packing up. Fancy some brekkie?' asked Uncle Pogo with a jollity that indicated he expected only a positive answer. Nelson sat up. 'I don't really like Scotch eggs, Uncle Pogo.' He yawned apologetically.

'Just as well,' Pogo chuckled. 'I ate yours last night. How about some toast?'

Toast. Even the sound of the word was delicious.

'I'd love some,' said Nelson, and his uncle's enormous head ducked out of the tent. Nelson arched his back and stretched his arms in front of him as far as they could go, turning his palms up as if he was trying to stop something coming towards him. It felt so good to stretch. Nelson had never felt so happy to be awake. That really had been a mega-sleep. He knew he'd had crazy dreams – he could still see the last few fragments of them in his head – but as soon as he tried to recall them in any detail they vanished. It didn't matter; those dreams had somehow left him feeling good. He patted his chest and felt the unmistakable bump of Celeste's pendant.

Just outside his tent, the toast was waiting for Nelson in a silver-foil parcel. Unwrapping it, Nelson found the bread had clearly been toasted and buttered days ago, as it was now as cold and hard as a roof tile. Nelson sighed and decided it would be best if he left it on the floor and pretended not to have noticed it.

Uncle Pogo had packed up just about everything. Rolls of plastic were stacked next to his boxy home-made electronics equipment, and the elastic ropes that had tethered the tents were lying in a pile. Those must be the snakes, thought Nelson. What a silly mistake to have made. The shadows and shuffling he had heard must have been Uncle Pogo trying to pack up without waking him. *Obviously*.

'Pogo!' called out a voice from across the crypt. Nelson turned to see a man, not much taller he was, striding towards them. He wore an enormous knitted jumper that started under his chin in a turtleneck and went all the way down to his thighs. It was striped with every colour you could think of and hung loosely over a pair of tight ripped black jeans and clompy army boots that had been painted with odd little doodles like skulls and spirals. His green-tinted hair was about normal length but had been pushed up into the kind of Mohican you can make yourself with shampoo when you're having a bath, and it was clearly a while since he had dyed it because only the tips were green. 'Over here, Doody!' shouted Pogo. The man met Nelson first.

'Eh, are you Pogo's nephew?' he said, with a West Country accent and a cheeky grin full of wonky teeth. 'What's your name then?'

'Nelson.'

'I'm Professor John Doodson, but everyone apart from my nan calls me Doody,' he said, shaking Nelson firmly by the hand. 'I'm from the Museum of London and I tell yer, Nelson, you're gonna be well famous, mate.' Before Nelson had time to ask why he was going to be famous, his uncle bellowed: 'Doody! Over here!'

Nelson always imagined professors to look like, well, professors: long white lab coat, glasses perched on the end of a thin nose and really hairy eyebrows, but after five minutes of listening to him talk about the history of the building and the significance of the room they had discovered last night, there was no doubt Doody was as smart as a fox and didn't just know everything about the history of London, he LOVED it too.

'He was on a roll, that Christopher Wren. There he was, in the middle of building this massive cathedral, and still he's got a million ideas buzzin' around in his head like bees, and I reckon this room you found was his little secret place where he could test all his ideas out,' said Doody, helping Pogo to roll up his cables. 'There's stuff in there, under those sheets, that I've never seen before. Amazing-looking things, but I've got absolutely no idea what they do. I'm hoping old Mr Wren wrote down what he was doing in some book or something, cos otherwise we're gonna be playing the weirdest guessing game ever.' Doody's mobile phone rang with the fastest techno you have ever heard, and for a few beats he danced to the music before answering the call. 'Y'allo, Doody speaking,' he said, and walked off to a corner of the crypt.

'You know who he is?' asked Pogo, with a nod of his head towards Doody.

'He said he was a professor at the Museum of London,' replied Nelson.

'No, before all of that. Blimey, I suppose you're too young to remember. Well, back in the nineties Doody was in that techno band, Messiaz. They were massive. You must have heard "Peace Out"?' Nelson shook his head. 'Really? I've downloaded his greatest hits into my leg. I'll play them to you later. Anyway, Doody was the keyboard player. He was a nutcase. Used to do this crazy dance and end up diving into the crowd. Bonkers.' Pogo laughed at the memory of Doody performing. 'The band split up years ago, but you wouldn't know it from looking at him, would you? I mean, he looks as if he's just about to go on stage.' Pogo had now reduced their entire camp into three plastic crates and two rolls of plastic sheeting. 'You know, what you and I found is a pretty big deal, Nelson. Who knew that fixing a leak would lead to this, eh?'

Doody finished his call by saying, 'Laters, potaters!' in a very loud voice, and marched over to Nelson and Pogo. 'The TV news guys are already on their way. Better smarten yourselves up, like. Yer gonna be famous, Nelson.'

Nelson knew he was supposed to feel excited about what Doody was saying, but he didn't.

Pogo took a look at his nephew and responded on his behalf. 'Listen, Doody, that might not be a good idea right now, him being on the news, I mean,' said Pogo. Doody listened as Pogo explained about Celeste's disappearance and how Pogo was Nelson's guardian until the family came home.

Doody frowned and shook his head. 'You're a brave little bloke,' he said. 'And when all this with your sister is sorted out, I am personally gonna make sure that you, and not this great plum –' he pointed at Uncle Pogo – 'are recognized as the genius who found Sir Christopher Wren's secret laboratory. All right?'

Nelson nodded and smiled. Pogo and Doody were looking at him like proud parents.

'Good,' said Doody. 'That'll impress yer mates, won't it?'

'Yep,' said Nelson, although his brain was quick to remind him he had no mates to impress.

Uncle Pogo took one last look around the crypt and then went past Nelson to pick something off the floor. It was the foil package that had contained a slice of toast, only now it was completely empty and ripped to shreds.

'Ah, glad to see you finally ate something,' said Uncle Pogo, and scrunched the wrapper into his overalls pocket. They all began to walk out carrying the crates and plastic, but Nelson was looking all around the crypt.

'Where's the toast?' he asked as if he was talking to a magician who had just tricked him, but Uncle Pogo merely patted Nelson's stomach and said, 'On its way to your guts by now, I imagine. Better get a wiggle on.'

As Nelson climbed the stairs with his enormous backpack pulling at his shoulders and a large roll of plastic sheeting under each arm, he took one last look around the crypt. It could have been a rat, he thought. There had been all those dead ones in the room he'd discovered last night. It was the logical explanation for the toast going missing, but it didn't settle Nelson's mind.

HIDEOUS FRUIT

The new day had filled St Paul's with light and life. What had been a dark and scary place last night was back to its utterly spectacular self this morning. That statue of the man on a horse was now free of its plastic wrapping and his stained marble features were being given a good scrub by a restoration team from Doody's department. Priests in black cassocks whizzed about the floor like battery-operated toys, and TV camera crews who had been told about the discovery of Christopher Wren's secret laboratory were now gathered on the front steps around Doody. No one had seen Doody since his band split up, so to rediscover him as a professor of history all these years later only added to the exciting story of Christopher Wren's secret laboratory.

There was so much attention surrounding Doody that no one noticed the tall man with the plastic leg and his nephew carrying the last of their camping gear out of the fire exit to a van.

As the van pulled away from the kerb, Nelson looked back out of his window and saw the bush his uncle had fallen into last night and noticed something very strange indeed. Faces. Ghastly little faces stuck among the branches as if the bush had suddenly produced a crop of hideous fruits. There must have been at least six of them, and they were all staring with wide, mad eyes right at Nelson.

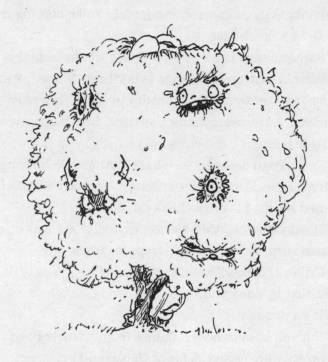

A passing bus wiped his view for a moment, and by the time he looked back at the bush the faces had gone, but they burned inside Nelson's mind with a clear and fierce intensity. The oddest part of all this was that Nelson had a feeling he recognized them from his dream last night. Feeling suddenly colder, Nelson quickly wound up the window and pulled the pendant out from under his T-shirt, gripped it with his fist and waited for that nice feeling it seemed to give him to come back and replace the chill currently occupying his bones.

'In one hundred metres, turn left on to the Embankment,' said a robotic female voice coming from Uncle Pogo's false leg.

'Satnav,' said Uncle Pogo. 'State of the art, this leg of mine. Does pretty much everything I need, except make toast and put the rubbish out on a Thursday.' He chuckled as the van made the turn, but Nelson wasn't really listening.

Uncle Pogo sighed. 'So what's that you're holding on to there? Necklace or something?' he said, and Nelson opened his fist to reveal the pendant.

'It's my sister's,' said Nelson casually, not expecting a gasp of surprise in response from his uncle.

'Crikey O'Mikey!' exclaimed Uncle Pogo. 'You do know what that is, don't you?'

'It's a pendant.'

'But you know where it comes from?' Uncle Pogo's eyebrows were raised as far as they could go.

'Erm, I think it used to belong to Celeste's mum. Your sister?' said Nelson slowly, in case this was some kind of trick question.

'Yes, but I bet no one's told you why her mum had it in the first place, have they?' He sounded a little breathless and Nelson shook his head.

'In three hundred metres, bear left on to the A40,' said the satnav.

Uncle Pogo snorted. 'Well, I'm not surprised. Your dad never did believe in magic and that kind o' thing after Isabelle died.'

It was true. Nelson's dad had always said that Uncle Pogo was as nutty as squirrel poo.

'Where does it come from then?' Nelson raised the pendant level with his eyes and admired its delicious strawberry colour.

Uncle Pogo took a deep breath, as if about to dive into a pool and then spoke in a voice that was much more deliberate and calm than his usual enthusiastic tone.

THE PENDANT
AND THE FIRE

'That little red stone comes from my father, God rest his soul,' said Uncle Pogo. 'He was a botanist – you know, studying plants, trees . . . nature stuff. Anyway, before the girls were born, he used to tell me stories about all the things he saw on his travels – plants that glow in the dark or can eat a monkey whole – that kind of thing. I loved hearing about it – like fairy stories. Then one day he came back from a trip to Brazil and told me he had found a secret jungle. He said it was like the real

Garden of Eden, and everywhere you looked were all these incredible flowers and trees that you couldn't find anywhere else in the world. Even the rocks and stones were like nothing else on earth – brightly coloured like gemstones. It was all because of a magic river that came up from deep under the ground. The River of Life, he called it. But here's the thing: not only did that water give all the plants and stones strange powers, but any little fishy creature that crawled out of it would just start evolving straight away, adapting to being on land. Same goes for any critter that crawled in – it'd start adapting to life underwater.'

River of Life? Garden of Eden? This was already the biggest load of nonsense Nelson had ever heard. He wished he hadn't asked.

'So then, when I was five, Carla and Isabelle came along. You never met twins less alike.

81

'Carla came out first. Big strong baby she was. Had a scream on her like a banshee. Then Isabelle arrived, and she was just tiny and weak, couldn't even breathe properly. They rushed her into intensive care and put her on all these machines. I remember being allowed to visit her. I couldn't believe how small she was.

'The doctors told my parents that Isabelle wouldn't make it past the weekend. There was nothing they could do. But my father, he wasn't having that. He went back to the jungle to find something to save her.'

Uncle Pogo paused for a moment. They were waiting at a red light, and Pogo glanced across at the pendant in Nelson's hand.

'A few hours later Dad came home with that little stone and he laid it beside Isabelle in her hospital crib – and the doctors said they'd never seen anything like it. Couldn't explain how Isabelle could suddenly breathe all by herself, her heart beating like a little drum. The weekend she was supposed to have died, Isabelle was back at home with all of us, gurgling and snorting away like a cheeky little piglet in my mother's arms. Dad had the stone made into a pendant so that she could wear it all the time.'

Uncle Pogo's voice trailed off as if he was lost in the happy memory.

'Wait a minute. You just said he went to Brazil and back in a few hours,' said Nelson, now convinced his uncle was making this up.

'Ah, that was thanks to the Bang Stone. He found it

in the jungle. Dad said if you swallowed that stone and thought of where you wanted to be – BANG! – you were there. That's how he got there and back so fast.'

'You saw him do that? Disappear, I mean,' Nelson asked.

'Err . . . Well, not exactly.'

Nelson stayed silent. This was exactly the kind of mumbo-jumbo parents tell children to cheer them up, and Nelson couldn't understand why even a loony like his uncle hadn't worked this out yet.

'But he really did go to Brazil. I heard a big bang outside the hospital and I looked out of the window. There he was – out of nowhere. Then he took something from his pocket and held whatever it was so tight and he was crying his eyes out. And when he had no more tears left, he opened his hands, and there was the stone.'

Not one bit of this was making any sense to Nelson, but the most confusing part of it all was that Pogo really believed this crazy stuff was true.

'I don't expect you to believe me,' said Uncle Pogo. 'Your father never did.'

'I do. I do. It's just . . . Well, you have to admit it is pretty amazing.'

'Yep. It was amazing. It was a miracle. Except it turns out you have to pay for miracles,' said Uncle Pogo in a dark tone. 'Dad said that the way the stone worked was that you poured all your love and hope into it and it could save someone's life. His love was strong enough to save

Isabelle but he was never the same again. He was like an empty version of himself. All hollow and distant, as if someone had scooped him out and left just the shell of him. It was as if he'd given all his love and happiness to Isabelle, see, and had none left for himself. I think that's why he died soon after.'

'But that's terrible,' said Nelson.

'Well, that was nothing compared to what happened to Carla. I mean, even though she was the prettiest and the smartest of the twins by a mile, Carla was always jealous of her sister. As they grew up Isabelle always loved to hear me tell the story of the River of Life and the pendant, but it just made Carla jealous. Jealous of how happy Isabelle was all the time. Jealous of the pendant and the love it contained. In the end, it drove her mad.'

' What happened?' said Nelson, who was now hooked into the story.

'When they were twenty years old they had a terrible argument and didn't speak to each other for years. Isabelle got married to your dad and had Celeste, and Carla got married to some guy called Brian. Then one day Isabelle got a call out of the blue. It was Carla. She said she wanted to meet Isabelle and make amends. So Isabelle went. She left little Celeste with your dad and went to see Carla. It was the last time I saw either of them.'

'Were you there too?' said Nelson.

'I was outside. Isabelle told me she was going to meet Carla, so of course I wanted to be there. But I was too late.

When I got there the house was on fire, and when I tried to get in a wall collapsed and fell on my leg,' said Uncle Pogo at exactly the same time as his plastic leg said, 'Take the next right and your destination is on the left.'

Uncle Pogo pulled over, gave a big sniff, wiped his nose on the back of his hand and turned to face Nelson, who continued to stare at him with wide eyes and open mouth.

'Sorry. That was all a bit heavy, wasn't it?' said Uncle Pogo, but Nelson shook his head.

'No, it wasn't. It was . . . yeah, it was a bit.'

'Well, that's all ancient history. Talking of which, I say we celebrate being the discoverers of the lost chamber of St Paul's!' said Uncle Pogo with his usual cheer. 'I have a ton of food in the freezer. I shall prepare you a feast fit for a king!' He heaved his great body out of the van while Nelson unbuckled his seat belt and tried not to imagine what frostbitten horrors lay in his uncle's freezer.

THE SCREAM

The meal Uncle Pogo prepared for them both was indeed dreadful. A lasagne bearing little resemblance to the delicious stuff Nelson was used to at home. The meat was a strange wormy-looking grey and tasted exactly the same as Minty's dog food smelled. The cheese sauce was a gluey white flavourless paste, and the layers of pasta were as tough to chew as a leather belt. It sat there on Nelson's plate surrounded by a moat of green, watery peas like the ruins of a tiny castle after a dragon had been along and burned it to a crisp.

Uncle Pogo had registered Nelson's disgust. 'Sorry. I'm not really used to cooking for other people. There's a fish-and-chip shop nearby. Would you prefer that?' Nelson tried not to look too excited about this idea, but Uncle Pogo chuckled in recognition.

'Two large haddock and chips?' he asked, taking his van keys out of a small compartment on the front of his plastic leg and rising from his chair.

'One's enough for me,' said Nelson, and his uncle laughed again.

'And ice cream for pudding. What's your favourite flavour?'

'Chocolate,' said Nelson, and his stomach rumbled in agreement.

'Won't be long. Watch the telly if you like. Bound to be something on.' Uncle Pogo went out of the front door and into the UFO mother-ship blaze of his security lights.

The *clunk* of Uncle Pogo closing the front door triggered the dog to bark like a nutter again. Nelson still hadn't set eyes on the animal. According to his uncle, it had belonged to a chaotic family who used to live across the street. The family had suddenly moved a few weeks ago, leaving the poor dog tied up in the garden (along with several mattresses, an old fridge and a punchbag). Pogo had felt compelled to rescue the dog, only to find the reason they left it behind was due to it being a complete psycho. After it had shredded some of Pogo's most valuable objects and bitten his hands and ankle at least a dozen times, Pogo had relegated the beast to the back garden, where it seemed pretty happy.

Nelson walked to the kitchen carrying both of their dinner plates. I say walk, but actually, it was more like wading. There was more stuff and clutter inside Pogo's house than there was in his front garden. Pogo had lived here for fifteen years, and even though the place had three floors, a big living room, dining room and three bedrooms, he had made his bedroom in the tiny basement so he could use the rest of the house for storage and workspace. Everywhere you looked there was something Pogo was either fixing or taking apart to get a better look at it. Old radio sets spread out in all their various pieces, vacuum-cleaner motors opened up for examination, and even computers were dissected. As Nelson scraped the remains of their ghastly meal into a flip-top bin he stared up at the walls, which were covered in African tribal masks, some of them as big as a surfboard, with surprised expressions on their faces and spiky straw for hair.

This is the view from the kitchen window into Uncle Pogo's greenhouse.

From the kitchen window he could see straight into the greenhouse, which was out of bounds due its being a miniature Amazonian jungle, as hot and humid as the real thing, complete with insects and a bathtub filled with tropical fish. On Nelson's tour of the house Uncle Pogo had explained he was trying to continue with his father's experiments with jungle plants, but by the look of things, his experiments weren't going so well.

After washing their plates and cutlery in the sink and leaving them to dry on the draining board, Nelson made his way back into the living room, past a fully functional red telephone box, an industrial sewing machine on which lay a half-made kite, and piles and piles of books, and more books, and even more books. Even though there was plenty here to keep Nelson's mind occupied, he sought the reassuring glow of the telly. As he waited for the screen to warm up, Nelson settled back into Uncle Pogo's large black chair, which responded instantly by massaging his back, neck and legs. It felt odd at first, but by the time a programme had appeared on the TV screen Nelson had decided he very much liked the feeling of being kneaded like dough. He scrolled through the channels, past a horse race, past a man holding another man up against a car and telling him he'd had enough of his lies, straight past a baffling commercial for something involving the woman from *Pirates of the Caribbean* and a motorbike, and then stopped dead at the sight of a face he recognized: John Doodson was standing on the steps of St Paul's Cathedral talking to the cameras. Below his face was a caption that read 'Prof J. Doodson. Museum of London.'

'The room, which we believe to be Christopher Wren's private laboratory, was discovered last night while repairs were being carried out on the cathedral, and in all my years of working for the Museum of London, I've never been so surprised by a find. I mean, it's amazing to think that millions of people have been in and out of this place and no one has ever known about this room.'

The picture cut to video footage of Doody inside the room as a voiceover informed the public that the team behind this discovery was led by ex-musician Professor John Doodson – former keyboard player in 90s techno group Messiaz. Meanwhile, Doody was peeling back the dustsheets that covered the strange objects and explaining what he had found.

*Here are some sketches of the things
Doody was talking about.*

Wren was working on a new kind of musical instrument – little wires that when stretched between the fingers vibrated hundreds of tiny tuned bells.

In order to meet the ever-increasing demands for huge wigs (extremely popular at the time), Wren was developing a tonic that when rubbed on pigs would make them grow masses of luscious, wavy hair in just a few days.

Caged birds were all the rage but Wren had been working on a special kind of bird seed that when fed to a budgie would would make it glow in the dark at night.

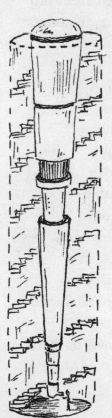

'We've always known Wren was up to far more than just building a cathedral,' said Doody. 'The central staircase here was originally constructed to house a telescope that would have been as tall as the cathedral itself. I mean, this was a man who liked to think outside the box! But what we've found here, well, we've never seen anything like this stuff before. I mean, look at this . . .'

Doody turned and the camera followed him to the sheet-covered table Nelson had stood on to reach the pipe last night. Nelson winced – his memory of falling back on to it was still fresh in his mind.

'This is an absolutely amazing piece,' said Doody as he reached for a tray of items neatly displayed on green velvet. Among the ancient objects were the seven copper vials. 'Yer see, Christopher Wren had all these ideas he was trying out.' Doody chuckled as he held up two of the copper vials. One of them had the word GREED etched into the copper; the other had the word ENVY.

'There are seven of these, one for each of the so-called seven deadly sins,' explained Doody as he peeled back a sheet to reveal the table Nelson had stood on last night to reach the leaking pipe, but instead of revealing a piece of flat wood, the table was covered in hundreds and hundreds of tiny needles – all pointing upward and arranged in spirals and intricate twisting patterns. Nelson's eyes widened. He clearly remembered falling on to that table last night. How on earth had he not realized it was covered in nasty-looking spikes?

'So the idea was, you'd lay yourself down on here on this lovely bed of needles – not exactly comfy, I'd imagine – and somehow these things would draw the seven deadly sins out of your soul and collect them in these copper vials, for safe keeping, like. Luckily they seem to be empty.' He chuckled, and the picture cut back to the newsroom to where the anchorman was enjoying a polite chuckle too. 'Professor John Doodson there, on today's incredible discovery of Sir Christopher Wren's secret test chamber at St Paul's Cathedral. And in other news today . . .' continued the anchorman, but Nelson's mind was off racing all over the place.

Why hadn't it hurt him to fall on those spikes? Surely it would have left him covered in cuts or puncture wounds? Nelson pushed back the sleeve of his hoody until it reached his elbow and turned his arm around. Nothing. His skin looked normal – not a scratch in sight on either arm. The news programme was drawing to a close.

'And now the weather. It'll be another rainy day for most of the south-east, with showers expected around noon and spreading . . .'

Nelson suddenly remembered the plastic poncho he had been wearing. Maybe it had protected him from the needles? It was still hanging on the banister rail, and when Nelson lifted it up for close inspection he noticed there were tiny pinpricks all over the poncho, making it utterly useless for the next time it rained. 'That's so weird,' said Nelson to himself, and just to be sure the spikes hadn't gone all the way through his clothes and stuck into his back, Nelson pulled his sweater over his head and yanked up the sleeves of his T-shirt.

'. . . Scattered showers for most of the north, although tomorrow should be clearer with the promise of some sun . . .' continued the happy weatherman.

Twisting his neck as far as it would go, Nelson strained to get a good look at the back of his shoulders, and just under the T-shirt he caught a glimpse of a patch of little red dots on his skin. Not a random scattering of dots, but a pattern. His neck protested – it didn't like being twisted like this – so Nelson gave his head a good shake before twisting it the other way. There was exactly the same pattern on the other shoulder too. All Nelson needed was a mirror to get a good look at his own back, but it seemed a mirror was the one object his uncle didn't possess.

There was a kettle in the kitchen. It was reflective but tarnished and his uncle had covered it in those tiny stickers you get on bananas and apples. Nelson peeled off as many as he could, gave it a wipe and lifted the back of his T-shirt.

'And finally, our top stories once again,' said the newsreader, turning to a different camera as the wall behind him lit up with images to accompany each story he recounted.

At first Nelson didn't understand what he was looking at because the kettle's distorted reflection made his body look like a long pink tube, but one thing was very clear: the bright red pattern that covered his entire back.

Pinpricks. Thousands of them. An intricate red tattoo that spread from his neck all the way to his lower back. And yet he didn't feel a thing, not even an itch. How on earth can you fall heavily on to a bed of needles that puncture your skin and not feel it? In fact, quite the opposite – Nelson clearly remembered feeling fantastic. How weird.

'As the search continues for British schoolgirl Celeste Green, Spanish police say they fear the worst . . .' Nelson's attention was pulled away from his back, as the news story seemed grab him by the throat and smack him around the face.

He ran back into the front room, and there was Celeste's face. Her big smiling face in a photo taken in their garden last year. Nelson could only manage a tiny gasp in response. His body froze, and time with it. As suddenly as her face had appeared on the screen it was gone, replaced by Doody talking about St Paul's again, but Nelson didn't hear a word he said. His sister's face was burned on to his brain with the word 'Missing' in large red letters below. He knew what 'fear the worst' meant. They thought Celeste was dead. The news was so awful that it sent a sharp stab of pain into Nelson's chest, right where his heart lived. He opened his mouth to cry out, and a blood-curdling scream filled the entire house. This wouldn't have been so awful if Nelson had been the one screaming, but the horrible noise wasn't coming from him – it was coming from *outside* the house.

UNINVITED GUESTS

The howling coming from outside sounded as if an entire pack of starving wolves had just found where the three little pigs lived. Nelson spun around, eyes wide open, staring at the front door, hoping it was just foxes – he'd often heard them squealing and shrieking in the middle of the night, but this idea was instantly shattered by the sight of several strange little figures leaping over the junk in the front garden. The doorbell started ringing over and over again and somebody knocked at the speed of a woodpecker. The dog went absolutely nuts, but even its incessant barking was no match for whatever was wailing on the other side of the front door.

Nelson backed away, tripped over a foot spa filled with empty pistachio shells and stood on the TV remote control. The TV switched off, a lamp stand toppled and fell as he backed into it, while the horrible cacophony outside grew louder still as more voices began to howl and screech and hiss and knock and ring and . . .

And suddenly everything just stopped.

Except the dog, who went on barking like crazy.

Nelson desperately tried to reassure himself that

97

whoever or whatever it was couldn't get in and that Uncle Pogo should be back soon, but this brief glimpse of hope was quickly extinguished by a loud CRUNCH from outside. The dog stopped barking.

The silence that followed was terrifying. The security light was out, the television was off and Nelson could hear his heart pumping blood around his body as if he had just run the Olympic one hundred-metre sprint.

Suddenly a jet of flames fired upward from just outside the kitchen window with the intensity of a rocket engine before dying out suddenly.

Again there was silence.

And then a burp.

Yes, a great, big, gut-rumbling belch came from whatever was outside the kitchen, followed by a plume of black smoke that rose up and drifted through the – no! The open window! There was no way Nelson could close that window now. The best he could do was retreat and hope he wasn't noticed. He crawled backwards across the floor, his eyes glued to the smoke drifting into the kitchen, until he hit the wall. No, it wasn't the wall, it was Uncle Pogo's red telephone booth. Nelson reached behind him and found the edge of its door. As he gingerly pulled the creaking door open, Nelson heard a whistle outside, the kind of loopy whistle you would do if you wanted someone's attention. Looking up, Nelson saw a tiny pink hand reach up from outside and grab hold of the windowsill.

'HIDE' was the only word that came to Nelson's mind (which is quite a good word to think of in a situation like this – certainly better than 'sausages' or 'rhinoceros') so he scrambled backwards into the phone booth and the door slowly closed by itself. He still had his T-shirt and the poncho gripped in his fists and, as the door shut, he pulled his knees up to his face and curled up as small as he could.

There was a kind of urgent scraping sound, followed by a thud, and then somebody (or something) spoke.

'Well, don't just stand there! Lift me up, yer great lump.' The voice sounded angry, and as if its owner had the most terrible sore throat.

'Ow! You are currently standing upon my nose!' hissed another. A struggle ensued and then a great honking noise, like a faulty bicycle horn, began blasting away.

'Oh, don't start honking again,' said a different voice, this one more like a sad and desperate moan.

Thud.

Another thud.

The sound of wings flapping filled the air and something obviously made of glass and belonging to Uncle Pogo was knocked to the floor and broken.

'Oops-a-daisy!' said a rather plummy voice.

A slithering rattle, like a snake, was followed by three more thuds to the floor. Whatever had been outside was now inside.

Nelson screwed his eyes up tight and wished that

99

Uncle Pogo would fling that front door open and chase away whatever was there.

There was a thump, then an 'Oi! Watch where yer putting them spikes!'

'Shh! Look. See? I told you this was the right house. He's over *there*.'

The sound of the voices approaching the telephone booth completely terrified Nelson. He could hear things pressing against the booth and the sound of breathing against the glass, quick and shallow like dogs panting after retrieving a ball. The strange voices spoke again.

'What's 'e doin' in there?'

'How should I know?'

'Ask 'im what 'e's doin' in there.'

'You ask!'

'Honk!'

'Shhh!'

Then there was a knock on the glass. Not a scary thump, but a very polite one-two-three knock, followed by someone clearing their throat to speak.

'Um, hello there,' said the plummy voice, the kind you would expect from the Queen's butler. 'Are you all right in there, old bean?'

Though his eyes were still screwed up tight, the surprise of hearing such a polite voice chipped away at the great slab of fear in Nelson's belly.

'I know just how he feels,' moaned a hollow-sounding voice as if about to cry.

'Big deal. We *all* know 'ow 'e feels,' growled another, with a derisive snort to emphasize its point, which was met with murmurs of agreement.

'Oh, please come out,' urged the hollow voice. 'We need you, Nelson.'

They knew his name.

How on earth could they know who he was when he had absolutely no idea who or *what* they were? Also, hadn't they just used the word 'need'? They hadn't said, 'We want to eat you, Nelson,' or, 'We'd very much like to turn you inside out and wear you as a hat, Nelson' – no, they'd clearly said, 'We *need* you, Nelson.'

For the first time since this terrifying episode began, Nelson experienced a feeling other than gut-wrenching fear: curiosity.

With absolutely no idea what he was going to find, Nelson slowly opened his eyes and peeped over the tops of his knees.

At first it was hard to see anything as the phone-booth windows were steamed up from the breath of whatever was panting on the other side, but as Nelson's eyes scanned left and right he began to see little faces moving beyond the foggy glass. For a moment he didn't know if he was looking at little people or animals. They spoke like people, but they certainly moved like animals. In fact, their enthusiastic snorting and snuffling and shuffling reminded him of the piglets he'd seen clambering over each other to feed from their mother on a primary-school trip to a farm.

'Shh! You're scaring 'im,' growled one of the creatures, and the group fell silent.

'Allow me to do the honours,' said the plummy voice, and the phone-booth door began to open. Nelson's eyes widened, even his eyebrows started to rise and blinking was completely out of the question as the door gradually opened to reveal a truly extraordinary sight. A bird-like creature stood before him, approximately half Nelson's height and covered in dazzling gold feathers. Its chest was puffed up proudly, its eyes were large and heavy-lidded and beneath them protruded a magnificent beak of what looked like solid silver. How any bird could move around, let alone fly, with a solid metal beak was anyone's guess, but there it was, looking like a gilded dodo, with the voice and demeanour of a waiter from a very expensive restaurant.

'Sorry for that rather messy entrance,' said the creature, as it swept one wing forward and bowed. 'We did knock, but it appears your servant is away at this time.' Nelson heard one of the other creatures hidden behind the phone booth respond with a loud 'HONK!'

'I go by the name of Hoot,' said the golden bird. 'And I can tell by your stunned expression you have never met a creature as handsome as me. Please, do not feel embarrassed. I am well aware that my looks are, quite literally, stunning. However, my cohorts aren't quite as . . .' His sentence was cut off by one of the other creatures rolling into view and knocking him right out of the way like a skittle. This one looked like a great pink sack of potatoes with tiny eyes, large hairy nostrils, coarse skin, useless stick-like arms, hands and legs, and a mouth as wide as an oven door.

"Allo, Nelly-son,' roared the pink blob, and there was loud cackling from behind the booth.

'My name Nosh! You, Nelly-son!' said the blobby thing with a big grin, stretching out one of his funny little hands to shake Nelson's.

Nelson's fear was shrinking fast and an overwhelming sense of 'blimey!' was taking its place. He held tight to the door frame with one hand and slowly stood up to shake Nosh's hand with the other. What a strange little hand it was. Tiny and hot, like a plastic doll that had been left in the sun all day, except this hand was very much alive, had a firm grip and belonged to a body that was as big and round as butcher's belly.

'Nice to meet you, Nosh,' said Nelson, which wasn't exactly true. 'It is totally mind-blowing to meet you,

Nosh,' might have been nearer the mark, but the fact that Nelson even managed to speak right now was a pretty good going.

'Look! Look! It's Nelly-son,' roared Nosh, and like a group of excited children about to meet Santa Claus, the other creatures hidden behind the steamed-up glass quickly assembled in front of the phone booth to greet Nelson.

It is very rare to see something you do not recognize at all, but apart from photos Nelson had seen of some bizarre luminous fish that dwell in the deepest, darkest parts of the ocean, he could not remember laying his eyes on anything so completely strange in all his life. In fact, it is time to stop referring to the things now gathered in front of Nelson as *creatures* because that would imply they were something Mother Nature had had a hand in creating, but there was absolutely nothing natural about them. They were not creatures. They were monsters.

And though they were all roughly half the size of Nelson, their height was the only thing they had in common. 'Dat one is Miser,' said Nosh, gesturing towards a blue egg-shaped monster that shuffled forward on feet that flopped like wet socks. Miser had long tentacles for arms, rough callused skin like the barnacle-encrusted rocks you find by the sea and a nose that started at the top of his head and ran all the way down to a small, pinched mouth, either side of which bulged two very shifty eyeballs.

'Master Nelson, 'tis an honour to make your

acquaintance,' hissed Miser, gripping Nelson's hand with his sticky fingers.

'Give it back, Miser,' said what appeared to be a very sad-looking cactus. Its bright green waxy flesh was covered in hundreds of spikes and its arms were long, thin and trailed on the floor like spindly branches.

'I have nothing to give back,' hissed Miser, and Nelson looked down to see another of Miser's tentacles had crept into the back pocket of his jeans and had lifted the money left over from the cab ride last night. Miser dropped the money back into Nelson's pocket and retracted the tentacle with whip-crack speed.

'Watch out for Miser,' said the cactus monster. 'Greedy rotter'll steal anything.'

'All property is theft,' grumbled Miser as he released his other hand from Nelson's, leaving a slug-like slime trail behind.

Nelson said, 'Hello,' and offered his hand, but the sad cactus merely sniffed and looked back at him with two sad eyes rattling around in dark, hollow sockets. 'Oh, you wouldn't want to shake hands with me. Look,' it said, and flapped its feeble twiggy arms as if to prove its point. 'Lucky you. You've got proper arms. Not like these stupid things.'

'What's your name?'

'Spike. I know. So *obvious*, isn't it? Wish I had a nice ordinary name like Richard or Steve.'

A horned beast with the angry red skin and hands as big as boxing gloves stomped forward on shiny black hoofs, pushed Spike out of the way and shook Nelson's hand, but only managed a grunt instead of a hello.

'Hi,' said Nelson, feeling the bones in his own hand being crushed by its powerful grip.

'Stan,' growled the creature.

'Hello, Stan.'

'Easy now, Stan old boy,' warned Hoot, and Stan backed away looking awkward and angry.

'Dat one is Crush,' said Nosh, and the smallest monster of the group rushed forward. This one had a ginger-coloured body shaped like a cross between a puppy and a foghorn. It bounded towards Nelson on round feet that looked as if they belonged to a miniature elephant. Its eyes were wide, it had big floppy ears like a springer spaniel, four little arms and a mouth like the bell of a trumpet. The little monster bounced up and down, honking like an old bicycle horn.

'HONK! HONK! HONK!' went Crush as Nelson reached down to shake its little hand. But all four of Crush's arms were already wrapped several times around his legs like jungle vines. 'Hello,' said Nelson, and Crush replied with an emphatic 'HOOOOONK!'

'That's all he ever says,' said Spike, rolling his eyes, but Nelson couldn't help finding it quite funny. 'Oh, you might like him now, but you soon get tired of it,' moaned Spike as Miser pulled Crush off Nelson's leg.

'Where Puff? Puff? Where he gone?' shouted Nosh, but Nelson couldn't see any more monsters.

'The last I saw of Master Puff was outside,' said Miser, who had found an old coin on the floor and was hiding it in one of the many pocket-like folds of his skin.

Nelson's brain was suddenly engaged. A flurry of questions rushed out of his mouth. 'So, who are you and where do you come from and what are you doing here and how do you know my name and—'

He was cut off mid-question by the sound of a car horn. Miser leaped on to the bookcase below the living-room window and peered out through the net curtains.

'Puff? Puff, dat you?' called Nosh.

'No! 'Tis the one-legged giant – he has returned!'

hissed Miser, and retreated behind an electric armchair.

'I'll take care of 'im!' bellowed Stan, pounding his fists together, readying for a fight.

'What? No, it's just my uncle!' cried Nelson, as the other monsters surrounded the front door.

His words had no effect whatsoever.

'This is his house!' he yelled and was again ignored.

There was a jangle of keys followed by the click of the lock and in walked Uncle Pogo carrying two large plastic bags filled with their dinner.

'Sorry it took so long. They'd run out of haddock so I had to wait around for a bit,' he said, walking straight past the growling monsters without a second glance. Nelson was utterly lost for words, but the monsters had plenty.

'Mmmm, dat smell 'licious,' groaned Nosh, his slobbery tongue hanging out as Pogo's carrier bags swung by his face and the smell of fried fish wafted through the house.

'Sorry, but would one of you remind me who the large fellow is?' said Hoot, now standing on the back of the couch and tilting his head to one side.

'The one-leg cannot be trusted,' whispered Miser, as one of his tentacles found its way to the mantelpiece, where it stole a silver letter opener and a medal Pogo had won in a rugby tournament.

'Miser's right. I'll squash 'im like a slug,' growled Stan, and Honk gave a short and rather squeaky honk in support.

'Please don't do that!' shouted Nelson, making Pogo jump out of his skin.

'Oh. Don't you want fish and chips?' asked his uncle, taking two plates from the draining board as the monsters began to close in around him.

'Are you feeling all right, Nelson?' he went on, in response to his nephew's wide-open mouth.

'Can't you see them? They're all around you!' said Nelson, throwing his arms wide.

'What are you talking about?'

Nelson opened and closed his mouth and found he didn't know how to reply. I mean, it's not often you find yourself saying, 'Your house is full of monsters,' is it? He felt something tug at his trouser leg and looking down he found Miser looking up at him.

'The one-leg cannot see or hear us. No one can. Except you.' That certainly explained things to Nelson, but it still didn't help him find a way to explain it all to his uncle. Then, to add to everything else, a great purple bear claw reached up from outside the window and grabbed hold of the sill.

'Something's out there,' said Nelson, pointing at what was now two large purple bear claws clinging to the window frame.

'Really?' said Uncle Pogo, turning to the window. 'You might have a point – it's the first time that dog's stopped barking.' He got up from his chair.

'No need to get your hopes up – it's only Puff,' moaned

Spike, but Uncle Pogo was already leaning out of the window.

'Dat is Puff, Nelly-son,' wheezed Nosh, as a seventh monster, a furry and very slow-moving ball of purple, flopped through the window and on to the floor. It looked as if someone had deflated a huge purple cat. Puff had fat paws, a soft pink nose and huge eyes that  were almost completely hidden under heavy purple eyelids. He yawned and revealed banana yellow teeth.

'Crikey O'Mikey!' exclaimed Uncle Pogo. 'Where on earth is the dog?' He craned his neck to see further into the garden. A ripple of giggles, cackles and laughter began to break out among the monsters. The purple monster, Puff, slowly opened his eyes and yawned again.

'What are you all laughing at?' whispered Nelson to the monsters, noticing that the only one not laughing was Nosh.

'It appears that Nosh has consumed the beast, Master Nelson,' said Miser.

'Nosh was hungry,' pleaded Nosh, blushing and turning the purple of his face a really peculiar shade of pink.

'What? You actually *ate* my uncle's dog?' hissed Nelson.

'Did you say something?' asked Uncle Pogo, but Nelson shook his head.

'Oh, dearie me. Was this doggy a friend of yours?' said Hoot with real concern, but this only made the others laugh louder.

'That dog must have got out over the fence somehow,' said Uncle Pogo, turning back towards the dinner table.

'Uncle Pogo – watch your step,' shouted Nelson, but it was too late to stop him from stepping on the great hairy blob called Puff.

There was the most humungous fart as Puff deflated under Pogo's false leg like a squished whoopee cushion.

'Oh, Puff! You wretched beast! You foul and odorous cretin!' cried Hoot, flying back to take a position on the banisters as a cloud of purple bubbles rose into the air.

'Run, Master Nelson! Flee before the bubbles burst!' urged Miser, but Nelson just stood there as the bubbles popped, each releasing a cloud of purple gas.

It was Stan who took control by charging at Nelson like a bull.

BLAM! He crashed into Nelson's stomach, knocking every ounce of air from his lungs. Crush had already reached the front door and flung it open.

'What on earth is going on?' exclaimed Uncle Pogo, as he looked up to see his nephew flying out of the front door, which slammed shut of its own accord behind him.

But before he could say anything, the smelly purple gas found its way up his nose, overpowered his brain and switched him off like a light.

'Uh-oh! Dat bubble fart gone right up da man's nose!' cried Nosh as Uncle Pogo tipped forward and collapsed into his plate, sending fish and chips flying in all directions.

SOUL DIVINING

Nelson banged on Uncle Pogo's front door until his fists turned red. 'Open up! Let me in!' he shouted, but it was at least six minutes before Hoot opened the door and Crush rushed out to greet him.

'HONK! HONK! HONK!' cried Crush as he clutched Nelson's leg and squeezed it with all his might.

'Sorry about that, old bean. Couldn't have you breathing in all that toxic gas now, could we?' chuckled Hoot, but Nelson wasn't listening; he was too busy trying to get across the living room with Crush clinging to his shin.

'What have you done to my uncle?' said Nelson.

'He's not dead, just asleep. All right for some, eh?' said Spike.

''Twas a ripe old stinker that Master Puff let loose from his derrière. Days may pass before the one-leg rises again,' said Miser.

'Days?' cried Nelson, realizing that there was now no adult to look after him. Uncle Pogo started to snore.

'Who *are* you?' shouted Nelson, and the monsters fell into a stunned silence.

'And what are you doing here – farting in my uncle's house and pushing me out like that?' he went on, trying hard to keep his voice from showing how freaked out he was.

'Is the boy fick or somefing? Don't he know?' grumbled Stan, but Hoot fluttered forward and spoke on behalf of the group.

'Dear boy, it was you who made us. Or rather, I should say, you who *crudely extracted* us.'

'Extracted you? From what?' said Nelson.

'Your soul,' said Spike with a big sniff.

'My soul?' said Nelson.

'Is 'e gonna repeat everyfing we say?' snarled Stan.

'Master Nelson is no doubt aware of the red marks on his back?' said Miser, now standing on the table behind Nelson.

'Oh, yeah. But I didn't do it on purpose. I fell on a table with needles on it. It was an accident,' said Nelson. Then he remembered Doody on the news. 'Hang on. Did you come out of that machine? Are you . . . ? Are you my sins?' It wasn't the weirdest sentence he'd ever said, but it came pretty close.

'Yes, Nelly-son! Deadly sins! Deadly seven!' said Nosh enthusiastically. 'I gluttony! Eat everyfing!'

'But I'm not a glutton!' said Nelson, choosing to forget how much lasagne he could eat in one go. He didn't think he ever did much in the way of sinning at all, but he supposed that everyone did, a bit. Perhaps

114

some people's sins might make for scarier, less ridiculous monsters than the seven standing facing him right now. He could remember studying the sins at school, and decided that Hoot must be pride, Stan was obviously wrath (another word for anger), Spike was envy, Puff was sloth (which is laziness) and Crush must be lust (which, when you're eleven, is mostly expressed as a powerful desire for things like football stickers or new trainers). Miser, who was still stealing as many knick-knacks from the mantelpiece as he could, was clearly greed. Now he came to think of it, Nelson could remember feeling most of these things over the last twenty-four hours.

'So did you not extract us in order to help you?' asked Miser.

'Help me with what?' said Nelson.

All the monsters (apart from Puff, who had gone back to sleep) groaned.

'Oh no. Please don't talk about *her*. It hurts too much,' groaned Spike, clutching his chest.

'About who? What are you talking about?' said Nelson, but somewhere in the back of his mind the answer to his question was already there.

'Yes, I'm afraid I'm a little lost too. Do remind me – whom exactly are we talking about?' said Hoot.

'Celeste, you idiot!' barked Stan, and all the monsters howled. In fact, Stan was so angry that he punched the nearest thing to him – which happened to be Hoot

– sending Hoot hurtling into a piano that had been stripped of its exterior and had all its inner workings on display. You can imagine the noise Hoot made as he hit it.

All the monsters howled with the same awful howl Nelson had heard outside the house before they had come in. Nelson too felt like howling at the mention of Celeste's name, but he managed to control himself enough to speak.

'How do you know about my sister?' he said.

'We share in your pain, Master Nelson, for we are born from your soul,' Miser wheezed, wincing as if he had just been punched in the stomach. 'This pain . . . It will not go away for any of us until we find her.' He seemed to be struggling to keep himself from toppling over.

'Find Celeste?' said Nelson, his voice cracking. 'But they don't know where she is,' he added, and at that all the monsters turned to look straight at him.

'We're wastin' time,' growled Stan.

Spike tottered forward. 'Nelson, your soul is connected to your sister's, and we're connected to yours. Until we find her, we'll all suffer this pain with you.'

'Stop da pain! Find da sister!' sobbed Nosh.

'But I can't,' said Nelson, becoming more desperate by the second.

'*We* can find her,' hissed Miser, and the other monsters nodded and groaned in agreement.

'What do you mean? How is that possible?' said Nelson.

'Divining of the soul,' said Miser, and the rest of the monsters nodded again.

'How do you think we found you here, in this house, in this street so far from where you left us?' said Spike.

'Close eyes, Nelly-son,' said Nosh, and all the monsters became still and closed their eyes too. The only sound was Uncle Pogo's snores into his mushy peas.

'What are you going to do?' asked Nelson, with a pain growing inside his stomach.

'To divine the soul we must focus, so we close our eyes,' said Miser, and Nelson obliged.

'Now we say 'er name,' said Stan.

As if under some kind of hypnotic spell, Nelson said his sister's name. At the very same time, all of the monsters did too.

'Celeste.'

It was very strange to hear eight weird voices speaking in unison, but it sounded harmonious, almost musical, like the final note of a beautiful song.

There followed a peacefulness that Nelson had not expected. It was as if all his thoughts had suddenly floated out of his head. He slowly opened his eyes to see the monsters standing as still as statues with their arms pointing in exactly the same direction. And they were humming.

'Ommmmmm,' they hummed.

'What are you all pointing at?' whispered Nelson, and all seven monsters growled at once.

'The way to Celeste.'

THE RIVER OF LIFE

In the entire history of Planet Earth, only three human beings had ever discovered this particular part of the Brazilian jungle, and one of those was about to appear. His arrival would take place on a patch of ground that used to be filled with the most extraordinary and colourful flowers but now looked as if it had been scorched black by fire. Even the trees surrounding this little clearing appeared to have been barbecued. The reason the trees were in such bad shape was because this had been the site of many explosions, and it was an explosion now that heralded the arrival of the human being.

The bang was tremendous.

Once the noise had echoed away into the distance, all that remained in the centre of the scorched patch was a cloud of blue smoke swirling ghost-like through the trees and a very large man dressed most inappropriately for the jungle. A sun hat pulled low over his eyes made his ears bend like tiny pink wings, and the belly bulging from beneath his shirt was large, pink and smeared in sun cream. Yes, this was the slippery giant we met at the very beginning of the story.

As the smoke cleared the man opened his bulbous white eyes and fell to his knees, grabbing his throat as if about to be sick. And then he was. But instead of a disgusting mess, a bluish stone plopped out of his mouth and on to the oily black ground. As the man coughed and spluttered, the blue stone trembled and fizzed like ice cream in a glass of Coke. Tiny bubbles rose from the stone's milky blue surface and the unmistakable rotten egg stench of sulphur filled the air. The man continued to cough while reaching into a satchel slung across his shoulders and producing a very old-looking clay pot into which he put the blue and seriously smelly stone.

This is a Bang Stone. Yes, it's exactly like the one Uncle Pogo said his father had discovered. What Uncle Pogo didn't know though was where Bang Stones come from, but I can tell you. They came about when the universe first began. As you may already know, the universe began with a very big bang, and if you imagine this big bang as a cake exploding, then the Bang Stones are like cake crumbs.

'Brian,' whispered a voice, and the man looked up with swollen and soulless white eyes. It was a woman's voice that had called his name. In fact, it sort of sang it, like a mermaid calling a sailor from the deep. 'Briiiiiii-aaaaaaan,' came the voice again, and Brian got to his feet.

'I'm coming to you, my love,' called Brian, whose monotone voice conveyed about as much affection as a zombie with toothache. He stomped through the jungle, his stupid shoes slipping on the black vines that criss-crossed the ground and his enormous goalkeeper-glove-sized hands grasping at branches to keep him from falling over.

'Briiiiiii-aaaaaaan,' came the call once more. This voice sounded sweet and hopeful and very pleased to see him, yet Brian's face remained blank as he came to a stop beside a pool that was about the size of a large garden trampoline. The water, if you could call it water, was as black as ink and surrounded by more burned-out tree trunks, that jutted from the silky black mud like huge rotten teeth. Brian dropped to his knees and his lifeless eyes gazed into the black water.

'I have returned to you, my love. But so thirsty. Must drink,' he said, drawing water from the pool to his lips with cupped hands.

'Yesss,' sang the ghostly voice, 'you must drink.'

As Brian gulped at the water, inky rivulets ran down his chin. It may sound disgusting to you, but to Brian this water was delicious. It not only quenched his thirst, it stirred a memory in his mind . . .

. . . Brian remembered when the water used to be pure and clear. It was the reason so many wonderful, spectacular plants used to grow here. This had been the River of Life. The water from which the very first organism on earth emerged and began to evolve into the creatures that now inhabit the entire planet. But all that ended ten years ago, the very second he lowered his wife's burned body into the water so that she could heal . . .

His breathing became deeper as the pond started bubbling and overflowing, for something was moving below. Brian instinctively shuffled back and watched as a truly hideous face, as wide as the entire pond, broke the surface of the water.

At first glance it looked like a whale, but its skin was as translucent and gelatinous as a jellyfish. As the black water drained away you could vaguely see inside the creature's head. Its veins and internal organs throbbing away, its brain suspended like a piece of mouldy fruit in a jelly, behind two very large and very disturbing eyes. They were disturbing because they were human eyes. They might have been as large as tennis balls, but they were undoubtedly human. Ugly strands of hair sprouting from the top of the creature's head clung to the side of its slippery wet face, and when it spoke, the words came from its revolting rubbery, toothless mouth, which contained a large black tongue as long as a surfboard and as floppy as raw steak.

This is what it looked like. Horrible!

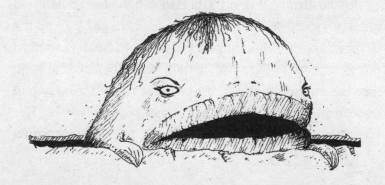

I know what you're thinking – how can a person, even a creepy guy like Brian, love a big ugly whale? Since when do whales talk? All very good questions. You see, this foul and blobby creature used to be beautiful and human and her name was Carla. Celeste's Auntie Carla, to be precise. You may recall Uncle Pogo telling Nelson how Carla had been very jealous of her twin sister for having been given the pendant filled with all their father's love. Well, that jealousy was the reason she tried to take the pendant from her sister by force. But as soon as she had torn it from Isabelle's neck, the stone had caught fire in her hand. Whatever magic had saved Isabelle's life had the reverse effect on Carla, who went up in flames, setting the family home ablaze too. But Carla possessed a means to escape the flames – her father's Bang Stone. You see, when she was a little girl, Carla had listened to Pogo's stories of their father's trips to the jungle with the Bang Stone, and she had paid very close attention. One day she had found the stone in her father's abandoned greenhouse, and by the time she called Isabelle to make peace, she had learned how to use it.

So had Brian. When Carla had caught fire, Brian had quickly swallowed the Bang Stone, brought her to the River of Life and laid her in the water to heal. It worked – she was still alive. But it took years before she even had the energy to speak, and in that time her body had transformed into that of a strange sort of whale. Her bitterness and jealousy had infected the water, turning it black and killing every plant that had formerly thrived upon that pure and magical source of life. Poor old Brian would have been fine had Carla not forced him to kiss her big ugly face to prove he still loved her. When the water on her lips touched his mouth it turned him into the sort of zombie who would kidnap a teenager, wear shoes on the beach and forget to rub in his suntan lotion.

'Did you find it, my darling?' asked Carla.

'Yes.' Brian opened his satchel and produced a tiny music box.

'Very good. Open it, Brian,' said Carla. Her voice was colder now.

Brian opened the box and a sweet little melody accompanied a porcelain ballerina turning around on a wheel. He pulled open a drawer at the front of the box to reveal the contents: a plastic fake-tortoiseshell hairgrip, several beaded necklaces, a couple of neon-green scrunchies and a tiny scrap of paper with the password to Nelson's family's WiFi written on it, but what Brian lifted out of the drawer was a thin gold chain at the end of which hung a lozenge-sized locket. Holding the necklace, he shuffled towards Carla on his knees.

'No! NO! This is *not* the pendant!'

'But it was in the box you asked for.'

Carla screamed like a banshee.

'I must have that pendant!'

'I have failed you,' spluttered Brian.

'There is still a chance. I will wake her. You will ask her where it is. And tell her. Tell her we will kill her family unless she speaks the truth,' said Carla with breathless desperation, before starting to convulse.

(This bit is really disgusting, I'm afraid.)

Carla's eyes closed, her mouth opened and she threw up something large from inside her stomach.

And suddenly Celeste's body lay in the black silt. The life jacket and clothes she had been wearing still covered her body, but her face glowed as white as marble under moonlight and her beautiful blonde hair was now a tangled mass of black.

'Where is the pendant?' asked Brian in his zombie-like tone. Celeste yawned and blinked so slowly it was as if she would much rather be back asleep inside the creature, who had now sunk below the surface of the water to watch.

'The pendant. Tell me where it is or your family will pay with their lives,' insisted Brain, rising to his feet.

Celeste spoke as if talking in her sleep. 'Oh no, please don't do that,' she said dreamily.

'Then tell us where it is,' said Brian in a louder voice than usual.

'My brother's got it,' she yawned. 'Just ask Nelson nicely and he'll give it to you. But please don't hurt him.'

'I have been to your house. There was no boy. Where is he now? Where is your brother?'

'I don't know. Nelson, where are you? Where are you, Nelson?'

Carla raised her horrible head and swallowed Celeste back down into her stomach like a dog stealing a meatball from the dinner table. I know this is all very odd, but what's even stranger is how comfortable Celeste seemed to be inside this revolting creature. It looked as if she was curling up inside a great big sleeping bag, except the sleeping bag was made of jelly and was actually a really disgusting monster's belly.

A silence fell. It felt as if the entire jungle was watching and appalled by what it saw.

'Bri-aan,' whispered Carla after a large burp, but Brian did not reply, as he had been distracted by the silver locket sticking out of the swamp mud by his feet.

You can see that one girl, Carla, was quite beautiful here with her dark hair and large wide eyes. The other girl, wearing thick glasses and braces on her teeth but with a smile that radiated pure happiness is Isabelle – Celeste's mum.

'She is telling the truth, Brian. The boy must have the pendant. Find him and bring it to me.'

'Yes. Of course. But, my love . . . if you take the pendant, are you certain it will not burn you again?'

Carla seemed to smile, although it could just have been trapped wind.

'The water from the river has made me strong and it will protect me. Now go!'

Brian obediently got to his feet and took the ancient clay pot from his satchel.

'Find the boy and bring me the pendant. Hurry, Brian! Hurry!' called Carla as Brian swallowed the fizzing blue stone, closed his eyes and exploded.

THE SPINNING BEACH BALL

Nelson and the seven monsters closed their eyes.

'Celeste.'

'Ommmm . . .'

Once again, their arms, claws, paws and tentacles pointed as one, but this time it was towards a beach ball that had a map of the world printed on it.

Miser was the one who had found the ball while searching Uncle Pogo's house for a globe. (He had also used this an excuse to steal more trinkets from Uncle Pogo's eclectic collection.) And now that ball spun around all by itself on the dining-room table. It was the sixth time they had repeated this exercise. Each time the ball had stopped spinning in the same place, with the monsters all pointing at the same country – if they really were about to set off to this location, Nelson wanted to be absolutely sure they were headed for the right place. It was, after all, a very, very long way from where Celeste had gone missing.

Nelson held his breath and waited for the ball to stop spinning.

Apart from the whizzing sound the ball made as it spun, all you could hear was the snoring, like distant thunder, of Uncle Pogo in the basement bedroom. Nothing in the world could wake him. Nelson had tried pouring glasses of ice-cold water in his face, but it was useless. Even when Nelson, Nosh, Miser and Stan had accidentally dropped him while carrying him to his room, Uncle Pogo's big old body just thundered down the stairs like a human sledge, coming to rest still sound asleep. Nelson thought it was a great shame that his uncle would not wake, because the prospect of embarking on such a tremendous journey with a bunch of monsters was even more daunting than being in one of Katy Newman's awful plays.

As expected, the beach ball ground to halt in exactly the same place as before.

Nelson and the monsters opened their eyes in unison and (apart from Crush, who of course just honked) said, 'Brazil.'

''Ow many times do we gotta do this before yer believe us, eh?' barked Stan.

'I just want to be sure, OK? I've never done anything like this on my own before,' said Nelson, and Crush hugged his legs and gave a very long and loud honk of support.

'Yer not on yer own, Nelly-son. You got us! We're yer soulmates, Nelly-son!' shouted Nosh, rushing into the garden having just eaten everything that was inside Uncle Pogo's bin. He gave a great burp and jet-engine-style flames blasted out of several black holes in the top of his head.

Nosh's belly was like a furnace where everything he ate was incinerated. This was obviously how he could still be hungry having eaten an entire dog only hours before.

As you can see, Nosh has little holes in his head like a pepper shaker. This is to let out the smoke and flames that erupt in his belly whenever he eats anything.

Miser was packing an old trunk with all sorts of things he thought might come in handy from Uncle Pogo's house, while Hoot polished his beak with Brasso.

'We know she's safe now, but for 'ow long, eh? Sooner we get goin', the better!' barked Stan, and the monsters began shuffling towards the front door.

Nelson looked back at Uncle Pogo's phone booth.

Should he call his parents? For a second Nelson imagined how that call might go . . .

HELLO, MUM. IT'S ME, NELSON. LISTEN, I ACCIDENTALLY EXCTRACTED THE SEVEN DEADLY SINS FROM MY SOUL LAST NIGHT AND THEY SOMEHOW TURNED INTO MONSTERS, WHICH IS A BIT WEIRD, I KNOW – OH, AND ONE OF THEM FARTED OUT SOME KIND OF PURPLE SLEEPING GAS THAT PUT UNCLE POGO INTO A COMA – BUT THE GOOD NEWS IS THESE MONSTERS CAN FIND CELESTE AND APPARENTLY SHE'S NOT IN SPAIN BUT SHE'S ALIVE AND WELL IN BRAZIL!

No phone call then.

Nelson would have to find his sister by himself. Well, with the help of his seven monsters.

'Nelson!' shouted Stan, and Nelson turned just in time to catch his uncle's van keys.

'What am I doing with these?' said Nelson.

'Drivin' to the airport,' said Stan.

DRIVING MONSTERS

Nelson sat in the driver's seat and stared at the driving controls. Due to his lack of a right leg, Uncle Pogo's van had been refitted so that the brake and the accelerator could be operated from a single lever next to the steering wheel, rather than by foot pedals. Forward to go faster, backwards to brake. Until now, Nelson's only experience of driving was several goes on the bumper cars at the funfair, playing the latest Grand Prix racing game on his PlayStation, and driving a tractor in a field at the end of the school fête last summer.

'Had to be a van, didn't it? Couldn't have had a nice car with proper seats,' grumbled Spike from the back.

Nelson turned the key in the ignition, the engine started and the monsters cheered.

'Wait a minute. Even if I can drive this thing, I don't know the way,' said Nelson, whose view through the windscreen was now blocked by Hoot, who stood on the bonnet having been voted out of the van by all the other monsters for smelling so strongly of Brasso.

'Map! You need map, Nelly-son!' shouted Nosh.

'I wish I had my uncle's false leg. It's got a satnav

and everything,' Nelson sighed.

'Ah, this leg you speak of – I may just know where it is,' said Miser, dashing to the back of the van and rummaging around in the trunk he had brought with him.

'Wait, Miser, you didn't steal my uncle's leg, did you?' said Nelson, turning around to see Miser lift the leg out of the trunk.

'I . . . I merely borrowed it,' said Miser guiltily as he thrust the leg into Nelson's lap.

On closer inspection Uncle Pogo's leg was even more impressive than Nelson had realized. Like an advent calendar, the leg was covered in lots of little doors, each labelled with what could be found inside. Nelson found the word SATNAV at the front of the leg, and as he pushed the tiny door it popped open to reveal a small and very thin remote control.

'Please enter your destination,' said the robotic female voice and Nelson began tapping at the keypad.

H . . . E . . . A . . . T . . . H . . . R . . . O . . . W.

'You have selected HEATHROW AIRPORT. Please proceed to the end of Box Elder Drive and take the first right on to Lemington Road,' said the voice, and once again the monsters cheered.

But now came the real test. Nelson was only eleven years old and about to drive to Heathrow Airport in the middle of the night. This is not only illegal, it's downright stupid.

Nelson pressed the pendant against his chest.

Instantly he was rewarded with a great wave of certainty, and without really thinking about what he was doing, he pushed the lever and the van jolted forward. Hoot fluttered into the air above the van and landed on the roof with a loud thud.

BEEP! BEEP! A red light flashed on the dashboard, saying that the handbrake was still on. 'Oh, I don't know how to take the handbrake off,' wailed Nelson.

'I'll do it!' growled Stan, promptly grabbing the handbrake from next to the driver's seat and ripping the entire thing out as if it was a bad tooth.

The van shot forward, clipped the pavement and narrowly missed a lamp post.

'You weren't supposed to rip the whole thing out!' protested Nelson, trying to keep the van on the road and off the pavement.

'Whatever,' growled Stan, clearly embarrassed, and threw the handbrake over his shoulder.

Crush jumped into the space where there had once been a handbrake and laid his head on Nelson's leg.

'Honk.'

'Thanks, Crush,' said Nelson. 'Just don't wriggle around or I might crash.'

'Turn right on to Lemington Road,' repeated the voice in the leg, and Nelson did just that. All he could think was, OH MY GOD! I AM DRIVING!

Exactly one minute and sixteen seconds after they had left Uncle Pogo's house, the orange car that belonged to

Nelson's neighbour Hilda Mills came racing past them. The small battered vehicle dragged its exhaust against the tarmac, screeched around the corner, drove up on to the pavement and smashed into the front wall of Pogo's garden. For a moment it just sat there, crumpled against the bricks and debris, hissing steam like a kettle. Then the driver's door opened. But it wasn't Hilda who got out; it was the great hulk called Brian. For a moment Brian stood in the glow of the security light, like a visitor from another planet, before he began walking up the path towards the front door.

By the time Brian had broken into the house and found it to be empty except for a sleeping Uncle Pogo, Nelson and his monsters were already on the A40 flyover and halfway to Heathrow Airport. Unfortunately, the computer on Pogo's desk was still showing the last thing Nelson had been searching for – flights from Heathrow to Brazil.

'For Heathrow Terminal 5, take the next exit,' said the satnav, as if this was a perfectly simple thing to do. However, for Nelson it meant swinging the steering wheel to the left and swerving slowly across two lanes in order to head down a ramp towards a roundabout. The monsters howled with excitement, extracted as they were from the bit of Nelson's little soul that secretly loved mayhem. Nelson had got used to the levers —it was the other cars on the road that were his concern. He was going slower than everyone else, which provoked a lot of honking of horns.

'Are we nearly there yet?' moaned Spike, and his answer came in the form of a 747 roaring overhead.

'At the roundabout take the third exit,' said the navigation system.

For Nelson, entering the roundabout was like entering a giant game of bumper cars. Sweat glistened on his forehead. He'd pulled his hood up so that no one would notice that an eleven-year-old boy was driving a van by himself, but that was making him hotter still.

'You missed the turning, you idiot!' bellowed Stan.

'Yeah, well, it doesn't help having you lot shouting at me, you know.' Nelson didn't dare take a hand off the wheel to wipe his brow for fear of crashing. The monsters cackled and scoffed as Nelson drove round the roundabout again, waiting for the satnav to tell him which exit to take. Unfortunately the instructions were interrupted by the ringing of the phone in Pogo's false leg.

'Oh no! I don't know where to go. Which one is the third exit?' said Nelson in his new stressed-out voice.

'This is Pogo. I'm sorry I can't take your call at the moment, but please leave a message after the beep and I'll get right back to you . . . BEEP!' went the answer machine in the false leg and then a voice that Nelson knew began to speak.

'Pogo? Mate, it's Doody. Look, sorry to call you in the middle of the night, but I'm in the Westminster labs and, well, we found some blood on the table with all the needles, so I wondered if either you or that little nephew of yours had fallen on it. It's just that the blood is fresh, so I wanted to check you was all right and not hurt or nuffin'. All right. Call me when you wake up, yer lazy so-and-so – BEEP.'

'Take the third exit for Heathrow Airport,' said the navigator, and finally, after ten torturous laps of the roundabout, Nelson steered the van in the correct direction.

'I hate roundabouts,' he muttered. They entered a tunnel that filled the van with orange light and the monsters cooed at the effect it gave.

'You have arrived at your destination,' said Pogo's leg as the van emerged on the other side, and the monsters cheered, but they hadn't quite arrived yet. Nelson had no idea where to go and arrows and signposts seemed to multiply in front of him like some kind of baffling card trick. He slowed right down, but a car behind him honked in frustration before pulling up alongside them, winding down a window and shouting something rude. Nelson kept looking straight ahead, hoping the angry driver could not tell he was a kid. Hoot had been flying low enough to hear and decided to show his support by doing what birds do best, which is pooping on car windscreens. If Hoot had been a normal-sized bird the driver would not have had cause for alarm, but Hoot was the size of a dog and his glittering golden poop was as large as a cow pat, which meant that when it hit the windscreen the driver screamed and had to make an emergency stop.

This altercation had forced Nelson to stay in his lane, which turned out to be a good thing as it led directly to the terminal for flights to South America.

Nelson stopped the van with one of the front wheels up on the kerb just before it hit a suitcase belonging to a family who were unloading luggage from their car.

He turned off the engine and sat back in his seat. They weren't even out of the country yet, but Nelson felt as if he couldn't possibly go any further, and had it not been for a traffic warden approaching he would have happily stayed in the van for at least another twenty minutes, just to get his breath back.

'Oh, great, now we're going to get a parking ticket,'

said Spike in his usual monotone, as Nelson quickly scrambled over the seats to stay out of sight.

Once the warden had passed, Nelson and the monsters jumped out of the back doors.

'What are we gonna do with the van?' said Nelson, but none of the monsters were listening. Miser had stolen the trolley from the family next to them, and the rest of the monsters were all loading the trunk on to it. 'Uh-oh, Nelson's gonna drive again,' cackled Stan, and all the monsters piled on.

'Excuse me, that's *our* trolley,' said the mother of the family at the next car.

Nelson looked awkward and opened his mouth but words did not come out.

'Tell her to get lost,' grunted Stan, but the best Nelson could come up with was a squeaky 'Sorry!' as he pushed the trolley as fast as he could into Terminal 5 of Heathrow Airport, with the monsters laughing at him all the way.

THE GOOD NEWS, THE BAD NEWS AND THE FIREBALL

First, the good news:
The good news was that a British Airways flight bound for Brazil was due to depart in exactly one hour and fifteen minutes.

And now the bad news:
Nelson had no money to buy a ticket, and even if he did have the money, he hadn't thought to drive home and get his passport, and even if he had had the money and the passport, there was no way a boy of his age would be allowed to travel on his own without the proper paperwork and a chaperone. They definitely hadn't thought this through.

What about the fireball?
That doesn't happen yet. But it will. Soon.

'Well, we're stuffed,' said Spike, who had been made to walk alongside the trolley to avoid pricking his fellow monsters.

Nelson knew he was right. They were stuffed. He

looked around and spotted Hoot perched on a huge illuminated billboard for a men's fragrance, which suited Hoot nicely, as he sat there admiring the perfect blond hair of the gentleman in the advert beneath his golden claws.

'If anyone could see what I can see, they would totally freak out,' said Nelson to himself, and this made an idea pop into his head like a slice of golden toast popping up from a toaster.

To everyone in the airport, this is what
Nelson's trolley looked like:

And to Nelson, this is what his trolley looked like:

Nelson could see the departure lounge where the plane was getting ready to board. It was only thirty metres away, but with all that security, it might as well have been a thousand miles.

'Can you make me invisible like you?' whispered Nelson.

'Don't be daft,' was Stan's response, and the other monsters snorted.

'You go in ma belly!' shouted Nosh excitedly, pointing to his bulging stomach.

'Actually, fatty's got a point,' said Spike.

144

'Ya! I hide you, Nelly-son. I hide you in ma big fat belly and we all go on da plane!'

'And I would be invisible?' said Nelson nervously.

'While it is true you will be invisible inside Nosh's ample gut, you would have very little time before Nosh's belly incinerated you,' said Miser.

'How long?' said Nelson.

'It depends on the size of what he has eaten. The bigger the meal, the longer he needs to generate the fire. My estimate would be around three minutes at best.'

'Three minutes?' said Nelson thoughtfully. 'That might be enough time. And you can definitely spit me out before your stomach catches fire?'

Nosh nodded eagerly.

'But what if he enjoys the taste of you, Master Nelson? Self-control while snacking is hardly one of Nosh's strong points,' hissed Miser as his tentacles picked the pockets of a businessman who was staring at the departure board right behind them.

All the monsters looked at Nelson.

'I think . . . it's quite likely . . . Nelson will . . . be cooked alive,' yawned Puff.

Without thinking, Nelson's right hand pressed down on his chest and felt the pea-sized stone against his skin. That reassuring wave washed over him once again.

'Honk! Honk! Honk!' Crush squeezed Nelson's legs together and Nelson patted his head.

'Thanks, Crush. I really don't want to do this . . .' said

Nelson, which was another way of saying, 'But I have no choice.'

The monsters cheered to show their support and, in a rather unsettling way, Nosh began to salivate and drool at the idea of eating a human. Nelson pushed the trolley to a quiet space beneath a staircase where the only people around were asleep on their luggage due to their flight being delayed.

Nosh simply opened his mouth as wide as a sleeping bag and Nelson climbed in. If any of the people around them had happened to wake up at this point, they would have seen the top half of a boy floating in mid-air.

This is what it looked like.

'OK, we only have three minutes to get through security before Nosh's gut goes up in flames, so you lot better go like a rocket or I'm going to be roasted alive and we'll never save Celeste,' said Nelson, and instantly regretted saying her name, as apart from Nosh (whose mouth was full at the time) all the monsters howled in pain.

The stench coming up from Nosh's belly was as foul as a bin that had been left un-emptied all summer long, but Nelson knew this was no time to be squeamish.

'I shall keep count of the time,' said Miser.

'I say, they have a marvellous range of grooming products in that shop over there. They even have a lotion that could cure you of those awful warts, my dear Miser,' said Hoot, who had fluttered down from his perch.

'Hoot, we're going for it, so stay close and – good luck,' said Nelson, and Nosh's vast mouth snapped shut around him like a giant clam.

'HOOOOONK!' cried Crush, hopping up and down on the spot next to Nosh.

'GO!' shouted Stan, and off they went.

'One . . . two . . . three . . .' counted Miser as Nosh, now swollen to almost twice his normal size, rolled on to the trolley and together the rest of the monsters pushed it as fast as they could towards the departure gate.

Nosh's eyes watered at how delicious Nelson tasted. To make matters worse, it was almost ten minutes since he had last eaten so he was extremely peckish.

For Nelson, this would be one of the most disgusting

things that ever happened to him in his life. It was not only sticky and smelly inside Nosh's guts, but there were all sorts of gross sloppy things that flopped against him like rotting wet sausages.

Despite most people in the airport being entirely preoccupied with their own travel, a luggage trolley speeding across the terminal all by itself was a jaw-dropping sight.

'. . . thirty-five . . . thirty-six . . . thirty-seven . . .' counted Miser as the trolley reached top speed, knocking any luggage or people in its path flying out of the way like skittles.

'Honk! Honk! Honk! Honk! Hooonk!' went Crush, out of his mind with worry for Nelson.

'. . . fifty-eight . . . fifty-nine . . . Two minutes remain – hurry!' shouted Miser, as the trolley smashed into the barrier to the departure gate. Nosh rolled off the trolley and straight into a young couple busy taking off their jackets, watches and shoes in preparation for the security scanners. People being knocked over by invisible forces isn't something that happens every day, and of course it provoked huge amounts of panic, screaming and rushing about.

'. . . one minute, twenty-two . . . one minute, twenty-three . . . one minute, twenty-four . . .' said Miser, his voice getting louder in order to be heard above the pandemonium they were leaving in their wake.

Nelson had no idea how long they had left. Being inside Nosh's stomach was like being in a washing machine made of rancid meat. Meanwhile the monsters were rolling Nosh along like you would if you were trying to make the biggest snowball you could possibly make.

'Two minutes!' shouted Miser, who for the first time looked extremely concerned. Nosh's eyes were starting to glaze over in preparation for his belly igniting like a booster rocket.

There was only one obstacle left to get Nosh through, and that was the metal detector. Unfortunately, with Nelson inside him, Nosh was too big to roll through and became jammed right in the middle of the device. Security guards had no idea what was going on.

They tried to walk through the apparently empty scanner to assist the passengers who had been knocked to the floor, but they were unable to pass, as if some kind of force field was stopping them. Of course, it was a monster with an eleven-year-old boy in its belly.

I suppose this is what it must feel like
to be a Scotch egg.

Nelson suddenly felt a great surge of heat all around him and a new smell joined the stink: it was smoke!

'Two minutes, fifty-six . . . fifty-seven . . . fifty-eight . . . fifty-nine . . . Time's up,' said Miser, turning away to avoid seeing Nosh's head burst into flame.

'Stand back!' yelled Stan, before charging at Nosh like a bull at a fat matador.

BANG!

Not only did Stan succeed in sending Nosh flying forward, he caused Nelson to be spat out of Nosh's slobbery great mouth, accompanied by a ball of fire.

(It would take an eagle-eyed security man called Jim Tindle watching the CCTV tapes later that day to see a brief glimpse of a boy appearing in mid-air as a fireball erupted behind him. The footage would be examined over and over again, and in the end it would be concluded that this must have been a glitch on the camera, as boys don't just appear out of thin air, and no one really liked Jim Tindle anyway.)

Chaos erupted as flames engulfed the security gate and passengers who had been knocked to the floor by invisible monsters got tentatively to their feet.

Nelson had landed only a few metres away from the shop selling duty-free perfume and realized he was completely covered in slobber. The slobber might have been disgusting, but it seemed to have saved him from being singed by the flames. Luckily, no one was looking at Nelson, being much too busy watching the fire that had broken out in the security hall.

Crush leaped up at Nelson and hugged him around the neck. 'HOOOOOOOOOONK!'

'All right, Crush, take it easy. You're going to strangle me,' spluttered Nelson.

The rest of the monsters surrounded him but said nothing. They were all in shock having narrowly escaped what could have been a very nasty end to their journey and an even nastier end to Nelson's life. Even Puff was panting hard, with a disturbed look on his fluffy face (though it was hard to tell if Puff was freaked out because Nelson had almost been roasted alive or because he had just run for the first time in his life).

'Oh no, my backpack. Damn. Must have dropped it,' said Nelson, and like a perfectly timed joke it fell from above and hit him on the head.

'Terribly sorry, but you dropped this back there and I thought you might be needing it,' said Hoot, and Nelson was grateful despite the bump on his head.

So many security guards were rushing to the scene that nobody noticed an eleven-year-old boy covered in clear gloop quietly making his way towards the departure gates.

PLEASE DON'T EAT
THE SOAP

Security men and women flocked in the opposite direction to Nelson and his monsters, who walked as quickly as they could towards the gate.

'What about our trunk and my uncle's false leg?' said Nelson through clenched teeth like a ventriloquist (so people wouldn't think he was talking to himself).

'The trunk is back there – we'll have to leave it behind,' said Spike, his stumpy little legs clearly not enjoying the pace of their march.

'I took the liberty of stowing the leg you speak of inside your bag,' whispered Miser, who needn't have bothered as no one but Nelson could hear him.

Nelson wanted to compliment Miser on his quick thinking, but there were too many people around to risk drawing attention to himself yet again. That's when he remembered that he was still covered in gloop.

'I've got to get cleaned up,' said Nelson, heading straight for a toilet reserved for parents with babies that was opposite the departure gate.

'We gotta get on that plane right now!' shouted Stan, but Nelson didn't stop.

The monsters followed him into the toilet and Nelson locked the door.

'I can't get on a plane like this. People will ask questions. Anyway, I don't have a ticket, and I'm not getting inside Nosh again.' Nelson sat down on the toilet seat and dropped his head into his hands. Crush honked and hugged his legs, but Nelson was too worried and upset to notice.

'I will acquire a ticket. But I will need some assistance,' said Miser, and Stan raised one of his enormous hands.

'Yes, I shall need Master Stan for this. And Master Puff.' And he left with a very sleepy Puff crawling slowly behind.

The door closed and Nelson pulled Crush from around his neck, took off his sticky jacket and began to wipe the gloop off with wads of paper towels while Nosh drank from the soap dispenser as if it was a delicious smoothie.

'Please don't eat the soap – you'll catch fire again,' said Nelson, but it was too late. A tiny flame, no bigger than that of a birthday candle, lit the top of his head. Nelson shuddered at how close he had come to being cooked and digested by Nosh's ghastly guts.

THE DISGUISE

Donna Gatsky was a woman with pointed cheekbones, pointed glasses, a pointed haircut, pointed chin, pointed nose and pointed shoes. She was famous in the movie business for getting her way by being absolutely horrible to everyone. I'm only telling you this so you don't feel too sorry for her when you find out what happens next.

As you can see, Donna is pretty scary.
What's even more frightening is that the
person she is shouting at is her mum!

Donna was about to board the flight to Brazil, but first she needed the loo.

Miser had been passing the time by picking pockets with his tentacles. This wasn't just out of habit – Miser was trying to find someone who had a ticket for the flight to Brazil. Preferably someone flying alone.

Donna stomped right past Miser with her steel wheelie case in tow, and Miser, Stan and Puff followed her into the toilet.

Once Donna had finished on the loo, she came out to wash her hands. In order to do this, she laid her passport and boarding pass beside the sink, giving Miser a chance to check the details.

'This American lady is travelling to Brazil on the very flight we need to be on,' he announced excitedly. 'Stan, prepare to catch this beautiful creature. Puff, pass your ghastly gas and send this lady into a deep slumber.'

Puff did exactly that and Donna flopped like laundry into Stan's open arms.

'Very good,' said Miser. 'Now I must take this lady's case next door to Master Nelson while you two find an appropriate place for the lady to rest.'

'I'm not dressing up as a woman!' protested Nelson, who had by now managed to get most of the gloop off his clothes.

'At least you can wear clothes,' moaned Spike. 'I can't.

They'll just get ripped to bits. I'd love to know what a nice coat feels like.'

Nelson stared at the open case and the pinstripe suit that lay folded neatly inside it. It was identical to the one Donna was already wearing.

'Yer look like a girl anyway,' said Stan, and the monsters burst into hysterics.

'Shut up, Stan,' said Nelson, who right then decided the first thing he would do when he got his sister back was to get her to cut his hair. Very short.

The suit fitted pretty well. Donna was only a couple of centimetres taller than him, so he just had to turn the trousers up a little. Then Nelson soaked his hair with water and allowed Spike to style it into a severe bob, using his spiky hands as combs. Then he packed his clothes into Donna's case, tried to apply her red lipstick to match the photo in the passport as best he could (while the monsters all chuckled at him), and then added the finishing touch – a pair of dark sunglasses. No one wears sunglasses in an airport in the middle of the night except rich and crazy people, but fortunately Donna fitted both of these categories, so it would not arouse suspicion.

The only problem was shoes. Donna hadn't packed a spare pair so Nelson would just have to keep his filthy trainers on and hope they didn't draw too much attention.

This is the drawing Nelson never wants anyone to see.

Nelson looked into the mirror. Instead of an eleven-year-old boy with one freckle on the end of his nose, he saw a very smart woman called Donna who looked like someone who always got things done her way.

'Nelly-son look like lady!' cried Nosh with a big laugh, but Nelson ignored him.

'Ready?' said Nelson.

'Ready!' said his seven monsters, and Nelson opened the door.

SING ALONG WITH HOOT

Nelson and the monsters thundered down the tunnel like a football team heading towards the pitch but Nelson stopped dead when he saw the steward waiting at the door of the plane. There was no way the monsters could remain undetected in there. They were sure to cause chaos within seconds, and then the plane would never leave.

'You'll have to go down with the luggage,' whispered Nelson.

'And you get to fly in the nice part of the plane, I suppose,' complained Spike.

'The boy is right. We must avoid the humans' carriage – this way!' said Miser, and with his tentacles he whipped open a door in the side of the tunnel and the monsters, most of whom were extremely cross about not getting to sit in the cabin, escaped through it. Except Crush. Crush gripped on to Nelson's leg like a toddler clinging to its mother on the first day of school and honked his distress as loudly as he could.

'Well, then you'd better not do anything stupid, OK?' whispered Nelson, peering at him over the top of Donna's

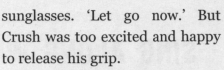

sunglasses. 'Let go now.' But Crush was too excited and happy to release his grip.

'Ms Gatsky, we're running late so if you wouldn't mind . . .' said the steward, who had short blond hair that was coated in so much gel it made him look like a Playmobil toy. Nelson just nodded and smiled without showing his teeth.

'How come that stupid honking little twit gets to sit up there with Nelson?' bellowed Spike, but none of the other monsters heard him over the roar of the jet engines or the wind that whistled through the metal bars of the spiral stairs leading down to the tarmac. Hoot instantly took to the air and drifted down to the door that hung open in the plane's belly while the others bounded down the stairs.

'Chop, chop! Get a wiggle on, my lovelies!' cried Hoot as the monsters scrambled across the tarmac and leaped on to the conveyor belt that was carrying the very last pieces of luggage up into the plane. The monsters surveyed what was to be their home for the next nine and a half hours. Spike let out a mournful groan; several of the monsters nodded in agreement.

'Oh, it's not that bad, chaps. Come along, chin up,' said Hoot as he settled on to one of the crates. 'I think it's rather fine down here. Plenty of room to spread out and all that. Isn't this fun, eh, chaps? All of us together on a grand adventure. I say, why don't we all sing a jolly old song? Come on, Nosh – you must know a good tune.'

To everyone's surprise it was Puff who spoke up. Puff hardly ever said a word, so when he did, everyone listened.

'Hoot . . . before we sing a song . . . why don't you . . . fly up . . . and look in through the windows? . . . Make sure . . . Nelson's on the plane,' said Puff in a slow drawl that was so deep you could feel his words vibrating in your chest.

'Spiffing idea! I'll be back in a jiffy!' squawked Hoot as he sailed out of the cargo door.

'But Hoot get stuck outside,' said Nosh, who had already eaten the handle of an old leather trunk.

'If I am not mistaken, that was Master Puff's intention,' said Miser, as the last of the ground crew stepped outside and closed the hatch. It was clear that playing a trick like this on Hoot was the funniest thing anyone could do, as the monsters began to laugh hysterically. Just so you know, the sound of monsters laughing is rather like the sound of the water from five bathtubs going down the plugholes at the same time, mixed with the sound of five lions roaring with satisfaction after eating a particularly meaty and delicious zebra.

Nelson had never sat in a first-class cabin before, and to say it was luxurious would be an understatement. His seat was as soft and comfortable as a feather bed and it could adjust into any position with just the touch of a button and the screen that rose like the arm of a ballet dancer from his seat promised him a selection of movies and games that made his brain spin with delight. Of course, Nelson was not alone. Crush was now snuggled up against him like a real-life cuddly toy. First-class passengers are also given lovely blankets and duvets, and Nelson used them to cover up as much of himself and Crush as possible. And he intended to remain under these blankets until the plane landed in Brazil.

Tap! Tap! Tap!

There were only nine passengers in the first-class cabin, and all of them turned towards the direction the noise was coming from.

Tap! Tap! Tap!

But there was nothing to be seen, unless you were Nelson, in which case you would have seen Hoot tapping on the window of the plane with his solid silver beak.

'HELLO THERE! JUST CHECKING YOU WERE ON THE PLANE!' shouted Hoot, although Nelson could barely hear him through the triple glazing.

'AND I SEE YOU ARE! VERY COSY INDEED! I SHALL NOW JOIN THE OTHERS! WE ARE GOING TO HAVE A SING-SONG! TOODLE-OO!'

And even though no one but him could hear Hoot, Nelson's cheeks flushed red with embarrassment and the rest of the passengers went back to their newspapers and drinks. The plane started to drift backwards away from the terminal. Nelson was just bringing his Coke to his lips when he was interrupted once again by . . .

Tap! Tap! Tap!

He turned to see Hoot waving a wing at him.

'I APPEAR TO HAVE BEEN LOCKED OUT!' shouted Hoot.

All Nelson could do was shake his head ever so slightly and shrug.

'OH, DEARIE ME! THIS COULD BE A PROBLEM!' shouted Hoot.

'Everything all right over here?' oozed the Playmobil steward, who for some reason had put on a jacket especially for take-off.

'Mmm, hmm,' said Nelson as his cheeks managed to find an even deeper shade of pink.

*

Though he knew no one else could see Hoot, Nelson didn't dare look out of the window again until the stewards started the safety demonstration. A quick peek through the glass confirmed that Hoot was perched on the wingtip. But beyond Hoot, inside the terminal from which they were departing, Nelson saw an even stranger sight: a very large man who had rushed to the open end of the tunnel they had just pulled away from was being held back by security men. The man wore a sun hat pulled low over his forehead, his tummy hung out of his shirt and he could not tear his bulging, milky eyes off the plane containing the boy he so desperately needed to catch. Of course, Nelson had no idea this man was Celeste's Uncle Brian.

As they rose into the air, Hoot let go and spread his wings wide. He seemed to be held in position above the plane by the jet stream that enveloped the tip of the wing like white ribbons made of air. And there he hovered, frantically flapping if he strayed out of position.

Nelson felt the plane bank to the right and there was London beneath him, just about to start waking up and getting on with things. The city looked wonderful from up here, with the sun peeping over the horizon just enough to light the tips of the tall city buildings like candles.

And so, as Uncle Pogo's van was towed away to a pound, and Brian was led off to an interview room for questioning over his suspicious behaviour, Nelson and his monsters sailed through the sky towards Brazil and a new chapter in their adventure. Nelson hoped it would go a little more smoothly than the last.

FRUIT AND NUT

In the search for food and clothing to keep them warm in the freezing cargo hold, the five monsters had ripped open much of the luggage belonging to the passengers in the plane's cabin above them.

The monsters didn't care at all about the mess they were making, they only cared about staying warm, fed and, most of all, curing the ache they all felt inside. The ache that would not go away until they had found Celeste.

Toothpaste turned out to be a favourite snack, but filling their mouths with toothpaste could not satisfy their monster appetites. They needed something more substantial (although Nosh was forbidden to eat anything large to avoid fires). Nosh suggested they try some of the shoes he was enjoying eating, as they were 'quite chewy and cheesy', but this didn't appeal to the rest of the group.

Upstairs in the first-class cabin, Nelson had just finished the most delicious feast he could ever remember seeing, let alone eating. Tomato soup with slices of oozing garlic bread, followed by roast chicken, peas and creamy potatoes, and for pudding a crème brûlée and a box of chocolates. He'd fed the complimentary olives and pistachio nuts to Crush, who now dozed contentedly beside him. Completely buried beneath the sumptuous duvet, the hum of the aircraft in his ears and a purring monster by his side, Nelson fell into a sleep as deep as the plane was high.

Meanwhile, back at Heathrow Airport, the security officers had decided to leave Brian alone for a minute to get a cup of tea and discuss how they could get this strange, silent man to explain himself.

As the security agents waited for their tea to brew, an almighty explosion rocked their offices, shattering windows and knocking people right off their feet.

It was a miracle no one was hurt, but harming anyone had never been Brian's intention. He had had only one thing in mind when he swallowed the Bang Stone: to be ready and waiting when that boy arrived in Brazil.

'Nelson! Help!' cried Celeste. She was hanging on for dear life to the open door of the plane, but Nelson could not reach her because his seat belt was holding him back.

'Celeste! I'm trying!' shouted Nelson as he squirmed to be free. 'Help!' he called, but none of the other passengers or stewards had noticed that the door was wide open and a girl was hanging out of it.

'Is the belt too tight?' asked the steward with the thickly gelled hair.

'Yes! I've got to get out! My sister! She's going to fall out of the plane!' yelled Nelson.

'No need to shout. It's very easy. You just lift this buckle . . .' said the steward calmly, but instead of releasing Nelson, he tightened the belt's grip. Nelson looked up into the steward's face and was met by a set of bulging eyes, white and watery like those of a dead fish.

Nelson would have screamed, but his sister had beaten him to it. She lost her grip and fell. Ripped away by the wind into nothingness. Gone forever.

Nelson woke with a gasp to find he was still wearing dark sunglasses and the steward with the gelled hair really *was* trying to tighten his seat belt.

'What are you doing?' said Nelson, which would have completely given away the fact that he was not an American woman called Donna Gatsky but a small British boy, had it not been for the fact that the plane was shaking wildly and the captain was addressing the passengers too loudly over the speakers for Nelson to be heard.

'. . . slight turbulence. Nothing to worry about. Please make sure your seat belt is securely fastened,' came the announcement.

As the plane lurched and shook, Nelson lifted the duvet to see if Crush had woken, only to find that Crush wasn't there.

The plane shook again and the overhead luggage compartments rattled and creaked as if about to drop.

This is bad, thought Nelson, who was still recovering from his terrible nightmare.

'HOOOOONK,' came the familiar sound of Crush. Nelson looked under his chair and there was the monster, rocking backwards and forwards with fear.

'It's all right, Crush,' said Nelson, but it was clear from the wobble in his voice he didn't really believe what he was saying.

The reason for the turbulence was chocolate. Fruit-and-nut chocolate, to be precise. Someone on board had a relative who loved it so much that they had packed twelve extra-large bars in their luggage. Nosh had discovered the stash and shared it with the other monsters. Not only did it satisfy their empty stomachs, it sent them gaga. They were bouncing around the cargo hold like toddlers at a soft-play centre. Nosh was rolling all over the place trying to knock down the other monsters, Miser was swinging from the ceiling and hurling luggage with his feet at Stan, who was punching each item as far as he could. Even Puff was wide awake and bouncing on a dinghy he had just inflated with one of his

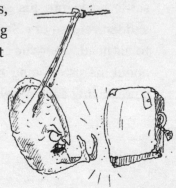

toxic farts. The only one who didn't really
join in was Spike, who was picking his way
through the luggage looking for slippers to
try on.

Though the captain had
clearly stated this was caused by
air turbulence, Nelson could hear the
unmistakable roar of his monsters
coming from below. From the
crashing and bashing he could
hear, he thought they might
be tearing the plane to bits.
And there was absolutely
nothing he could do but
settle back into his seat and clutch the pendant. The
sudden release of calm he craved spread from his heart
to his head, where he concentrated very hard on thinking
about his sister being alive and not on the monsters who
were having a party below.

THE POWER OF CRUSH

Nelson was desperate to get out of Donna Gatsky's clothes and wipe that awful waxy red lipstick off, but it would have to wait until they were safely out of the airport at Rio. As he followed the other first-class passengers through the icy air-conditioned corridors, Nelson remembered he was an eleven-year-old boy and that anyone checking Donna Gatsky's passport was bound to notice this. The entire journey would have been for nothing. He might even be arrested. Would that mean prison?

Nelson pressed the pendant against his chest and took a deep breath. The fear subsided like a wave gently receding from the shore, but the reality of passport control still lay ahead. Nelson joined the queue and opened Donna's passport. She had a severe face and her nostrils flared as if there was a bad smell under her pointed nose. Her eyes were blue while his were brown, but at least he had got the hair right.

Nelson copied what he saw the other passengers doing, and when it came to his turn he stepped straight up to the passport booth, where a large woman in a black police-style uniform sat behind a Plexiglas screen and laid Donna's passport before her.

The woman said something in Portuguese and then pointed to Nelson's sunglasses. 'Sunglasses – you no wear.'

There was no other option open to Nelson. Crush let go of his leg and ran around to the other side of the booth, as if hiding from the inevitable storm about to break.

Nelson thought of the photo of Donna and flared his nostrils as he lifted the sunglasses from his eyes.

Oh dear.

It was quite clear that Nelson looked nothing like Donna Gatsky.

This was it.

The end of the line.

However, the large woman's eyes suddenly glazed over and she turned to her computer and typed frantically into an Internet search engine. Nelson assumed this was a very bad sign, but it wasn't at all. The reason for her change in behaviour was Crush. He was gripping her leg beneath her desk, and in that moment the passport officer was overcome by an uncontrollable urge to have what she desired, and what this lady desired more than anything was a pair of black boots she had seen online that morning before coming to work. Thanks to Crush she *had to have those boots*. Right now! The feeling was so powerful it eclipsed all rational thinking.

Until now, Crush had been an adorable though fairly useless member of the group, but transferring his almost insane desire for things to this lady was a masterstroke. The poor woman had tears of joy welling in her eyes as she grabbed her credit card and typed in the details. Soon those boots would be hers and she would be the happiest human on earth!

Nelson watched, baffled, as she completed the transaction, jumped out of her seat with a great 'Whoop!' and ran from her booth, leaving all of her belongings behind, in order to get home and wait for delivery.

Of course, all this meant that Nelson was able to put his sunglasses back on and casually walk through to the luggage-reclaim area.

Nelson had no idea how Crush had helped him, but was sure the monster must have had something to do with it.

Nelson joined his fellow passengers waiting around a luggage conveyor belt. The other monsters would follow the luggage from the plane in order to find him, so staying put seemed like a very good idea.

A bell rang and an orange light began to flash at the top of the conveyor belt. A few boxes printed with the words HANDLE WITH CARE were first to appear. They looked badly bashed, and the noise they made clearly indicated they had been handled with the opposite of care. Then, to the horror of everyone waiting, a steady stream of broken luggage spewed on to the conveyor belt and a great deal of loose underpants, swimming shorts and T-shirts met their mortified owners. Nelson had an awful feeling that he was responsible for all the unhappiness breaking out around him.

As complaints began to ring out, Nelson was relieved to see six monsters tumbling on to the conveyor.

'Nelly-son!' shouted Nosh, and Nelson couldn't help but smile at the sight of his ludicrous gang. They all leaped off the luggage belt and surrounded Nelson with great relief.

'Just stay close and keep moving,' whispered Nelson, as he turned and headed straight for the exit, where he was about to discover two men were already waiting for him.

HELLO, MY NAME IS JESUS

Towards the exit of the arrivals hall stood a group of drivers wearing sunglasses and slightly-too-big-for-them suits and holding handwritten name cards. One held a card with the name 'DONNA GATSKY' scrawled in black felt-tip pen.

'Look! A driver with a car! What luck!' hissed Miser, as his tentacles scavenged the pockets of people distracted by waiting for their friends and family to appear.

'I am not getting in a stranger's car,' whispered Nelson through gritted teeth. 'Keep walking straight out of the airport.' They were halfway to the exit doors when the stink of rotten eggs hit them.

'Yuck! Was that you, Puff?' wailed Spike, covering his nostrils.

'Phwoar! Puff, you scumbag,' groaned Stan, and the others joined in with a chorus of insults. Hoot even faltered in mid-air due to the intoxicating whiff.

'It's . . . not me! It's coming . . . from over . . . there,' said Puff, pointing to a crowd of people who were holding their noses and trying to get as far away from something as possible. As they cleared the area, the source of the stink was revealed: standing very still, and dressed in his usual inappropriate clothes, was Brian. Nelson instantly recognized him as the man he'd seen at Heathrow, but what chilled him to the bone was the torn piece of cardboard Brian was holding in his big hands. Scrawled upon it in crayon was his name: NELSON GREEN.

'We have to go. We have to go quickly,' said Nelson, and he turned to wave at Donna Gatsky's driver. The man nodded back and reached out his hand to take Nelson's case. Nelson flared his nostrils like in Donna's passport photo and then shook his head to say, 'No, thanks, I'll carry my own bags.'

Nelson followed the driver as if this was all perfectly normal, but he could not shake off the feeling that there was something very wrong about that man with the sign with his name. Why on earth would anyone be waiting for him here, let alone someone he didn't even know? And how had he got here quicker than they had?

Rio was insanely hot and bright enough to make Nelson squint, even through Donna Gatsky's sunglasses. The driver opened the back door to a long, black limousine.

'Big car!' shouted Nosh.

'Oh, now *this* mode of transport is very me,' said Hoot.

'Shut up and get in!' shouted Stan, and the monsters ran ahead of Nelson, who had stalled on purpose to let them in first. The driver had been too busy answering a text message from his boss to notice his car rocking as seven monsters climbed aboard.

Nelson didn't want to be Donna Gatsky any more. He didn't want to get in a car with someone he didn't know. He just wanted to find his sister and go right back home again.

He would have stood there debating his next move for longer had he not turned around. One simple twist of his neck was all it took to change his fate, for it just so happened that Brian had been looking out of the window at the same moment, and his big, gluey eyes noticed an oddly small lady in a suit quickly look away. That quick, frightened little turn of Nelson's head was the giveaway. Brian ran towards the exit doors, barging people and luggage trolleys out of his way while Nelson dived into the limo and the driver raised his eyebrows in surprise before closing the door. The man had never seen anyone so keen to get in his car before.

The passenger area of the limousine was big enough to have two large, leather sofas facing each other, drinks cabinets down either side, a TV, DVD player, and a velvet ceiling covered in little white lights like stars.

'Dis a big car, Nelly-son!' cried Nosh, who had already licked the armrest and decided that when no one was looking, he would definitely be eating it.

Nelson looked out of the tinted window to see the strange man with the bulgy white eyes running after the limo as it pulled away.

'That man! Look!' shouted Nelson. 'I don't know who he is, but he was after me. He had a card with my name on it and . . .' Nelson trailed off because the man had given up chasing the car and was now standing in the middle of the road just staring at it, traffic screeching to a halt behind him to avoid running him over.

There was a loud buzzing noise, and Nelson turned to see the tinted partition that separated him from the driver lowering.

'Hello. My name is Jesus,' croaked the man.

I should like to remind you that people in Brazil speak Portuguese – and when you see the name 'Jesus' (which is as common a name in Brazil as John is in England) you have to say it like this, 'Hay-zoose.'

Jesus was huge. He had been a world-champion kick-boxer until three years ago, when an opponent kicked him in the throat and he had all but lost his voice for good. His massive body was topped by a completely bald head, a broken nose and two pairs of glasses (his driving glasses and, directly on top of them, his extra large sunglasses). Jesus was now a driver for a major Hollywood studio, and it was his job to deliver Donna Gatsky straight to the movie. Little did Jesus know that he would not be going anywhere near the film set today.

THE EMPTY HEAD

'Can you just stop mucking about with everything, please? We have to get out of this car,' Nelson hissed to his monsters, most of whom were sticking their heads out of the window or the sunroof and howling at the hot world zooming by. Miser was busy stealing everything he could get his tentacles on from the mini-bar – Nelson noticed that his body was now covered in various-sized lumps and bumps. He was clearly hoarding an awful lot of stolen goods in those strange pockets in his skin.

'Look, we have to find my sister, and we are stuck in a car going the wrong way right now!' said Nelson through gritted teeth. Miser pressed one of the buttons and lowered the glass partition behind Jesus's head.

'What are you doing?' whispered Nelson, and Miser flexed his tentacles eagerly.

'A car and a driver – a fortuitous turn of events, wouldn't you agree?' said Miser. 'Spike, would you be so kind as to take control of our driver?' Spike sighed.

'Oh, do I have to? It hurts,' said Spike.

'I'll do it, yer whinger,' snapped Stan, reaching over and plucking a cactus needle out of Spike's arm. A jet of water instantly sprang from the hole it left behind.

'Ow! See? That did really hurt,' said Spike, holding the sore spot on his arm.

'Big baby,' muttered Stan, giving the cactus needle to Miser. By now the rest of the monsters had stopped mucking about to watch.

'Behold,' said Miser, 'we will now make Jesus as empty-headed as Master Spike,' and stuck the cactus needle into the back of Jesus's big, bald head.

'NO!' shouted Nelson, but it was too late: Jesus was already slowing to a stop in the middle of a motorway. But the man didn't cry out; he simply slumped forward as if he was a toy whose batteries had run down.

'Someone's going to smash into us!' shouted Nelson as he looked out of the back window and winced as a small van swerved suddenly to avoid them.

'It's all right for you lot. You can just sit there. I have to do all the work now,' moaned Spike, climbing through the partition and sitting next to Jesus.

Outside, cars, trucks and vans honked and screeched their brakes and shouted in anger and fear at this stupid driver who had parked his limo in the middle of the motorway. All Nelson could do was hold his breath, clench his teeth and pray no one hit them.

One of Spike's biggest problems was that he was so full of envy that he always felt empty inside, and, apart from water, he was. However, he could transfer that emptiness into any living thing by sticking one of his needles into them. Once someone is empty, they are easily led. Nelson wished Spike had thought to mention this when they were at the airport, but never mind.

Spike turned to face Jesus. 'Nod if you can hear me, Jesus,' said Spike, and Jesus nodded obediently.

'Great. So, I am your new master and you will go where I want you to go,' said Spike; and again Jesus nodded.

There was a loud bang and the limo lurched forward and over to the side of the motorway. They had been clipped by a car that was now pulling in ahead of them.

The driver of the car jumped out and stormed angrily towards the limo. Nelson could almost see steam coming out of the angry driver's ears.

'We must close our eyes . . .' hissed Miser, and the monsters all did as he said.

'Nelly-son, shut eyes,' whispered Nosh, and Nelson pretended to close them, then opened them again, because he didn't want to take his eyes off the furious driver approaching them.

'We say her name,' said Miser, and on the count of three they all did as instructed.

'Celeste.'

Just as before, the monsters' arms shot up and all pointed in one direction.

'Ommmmmm,' hummed the monsters.

'Jesus,' said Spike, 'take us to Celeste.'

Jesus opened his eyes very wide as if he'd just been stung by a bee, and he threw the car into gear and pressed his foot down on the accelerator.

The angry driver leaped out of the limo's path and shouted something that, even in a language Nelson didn't understand, sounded very rude indeed.

While the monsters remained frozen with their arms pointed towards the right-hand side of the car, Jesus turned the wheel to the right and began to drive at full speed in this direction. This would not have been so bad had there been a road there, but as there wasn't he barged straight through a low wooden fence and continued across an empty field.

Nelson was the only one of the group who was not in a trance. Instead he could only watch with every muscle in his body as tense as the strings of a tennis racquet as they bounced their way across the field towards a dirt track heading west.

THE END OF THE ROAD

It had taken Nelson a while to get used to being driven in a stretch limousine by a man who was being controlled telepathically by a cactus-shaped monster, but by the time they were an hour into the high-speed journey, and with his old clothes back on, free of lipstick and with hot, thrilling air filling his lungs, Nelson felt absolutely certain that every inch they travelled was an inch closer to Celeste.

DRIIING! DRIIING!

Nelson ducked back into the limo, where Uncle Pogo's leg was ringing.

DRIIING! DRIIING!

The monsters remained completely oblivious to the phone ringing. They were still humming away in the trance-like state that allowed them to find Celeste – their arms pointed in exactly the same direction and vibrating as if an electric current was passing through their very strange little bodies.

'This is Pogo. I'm sorry I can't take your call at the moment, but please leave a message after the beep and I'll get right back to you – 'BEEP!' said his uncle's recorded voice and then Nelson's father spoke.

'Pogo? It's me. Stephen. I tried you at the house but you weren't there and I just wanted to know if Nelson was all right . . .'

Nelson was so happy to hear his father he hit the ANSWER button and caught his father just before he hung up.

'Dad!'

'Nelson? Oh my goodness. What are you doing answering your uncle's leg?'

'Dad, you don't have to worry, I'm completely fine. In fact, everything's great,' said Nelson, and then suddenly realized how stupid that sounded. As far as his parents were concerned, his sister was missing, presumed dead – you can't get much further from great than that.

'Oh! Well, that's good. Where are you? The ring sounded like a foreign tone,' said his father, in the voice of a completely exhausted human being.

Nelson hit the button to close the sunroof. 'I'm watching telly. But I'm all right, Dad. Uncle Pogo is just, erm, taking a nap. Uh, how are you?' Nelson was now wishing he'd never answered the darn phone in the first place.

'It's not good news, I'm afraid . . .' said his father, and Nelson instinctively clutched at the pendant.

'The police here . . . they've been very helpful . . . I mean, they've done everything they can . . .'

Nelson opened his mouth to say something that would

give his father the same certainty that he felt in his bones. But at that very moment a truck slammed into the side of the limo with the force of a tank.

BLAM!

The monsters snapped out of their trance as they were hurled against the side of the limo interior, and the call from Nelson's father cut off the very second the plastic leg collided with Nosh's fat face.

Before anyone could even say 'Ouch!' the truck hit the left side of the limo again, and everyone and everything inside was flung to the right.

Spike shouted, 'Speed up, Jesus!' Which Jesus did, allowing them to avoid the third collision the truck had been going for.

'What's happening?' yelled Nelson, but the monsters were in too much of a panic to make sense of anything. Nelson looked out of the rear window, which was now cracked in a cobweb pattern, and saw the truck gaining on them.

'It's going to hit us again!' shouted Nelson, and turned around to see Stan punch the entire sunroof into the air and then leap up through the hole.

The angry monster landed on the roof of the limo and turned to face the approaching truck. 'Let him catch up!' he yelled over the roar of wind and motor engines being pushed to their limit.

'What are you gonna do?' called Nelson.

'Whatever yer do, don't stop!' bellowed Stan to Jesus,

and with that he launched his fierce red body into the air. For a moment, his legs and arms whirled around as if he was running on air, before he slammed on to the bonnet of the truck. The metal beneath his hoofs buckled like tin foil and Stan took a moment to steady himself then pulled back a clenched fist that he clearly intended to go straight through the windscreen. The driver had no idea there was anything standing in front of him, but whipped the steering wheel hard to the right to avoid a rock in the road, sending Stan flying.

Stan managed to grab the wing mirror on the passenger side, but this snapped off and it tumbled into the road, taking Stan with it.

'STAN!' shouted Nelson, but the monster was already just a cloud of dust in the distance.

Just then the sun's rays fell on the horrible face that belonged to Brian, and Nelson realized who was trying to kill them. What he didn't know was why.

'CHARGE!' shouted Miser, and he led Crush and Hoot out of the sunroof.

'Wait! Don't be stupid!' cried Nelson, even though he knew no one was listening to him.

Crush leaped through the air and hit the truck windscreen like a gigantic bug. The glass shattered on impact and Crush tumbled on to the passenger seat.

'HONK!'

At that exact moment, Hoot flew back into view,

carrying Miser in his claws. As he swooped over the truck, Hoot dropped Miser like a bomb on to the roof.

BLAM!

Miser's tentacles whipped out from either side of him and gripped the top of the driver's cabin. Miser took as many steps backwards as he could before pinging himself forward like a catapult, looping back and crashing through the windscreen.

'HONK! HONK!'

Crush was really too small to be much use in a fight against a very large zombified man, but Miser was able to slap Brian silly with the whip-crack of his tentacles. Of course, Brian couldn't see the monsters, but he could certainly feel the sharp stinging pain of their punches, kicks and slaps. With one hand on the steering wheel, he beat the air around him with his other fist in the hope it would connect with whatever was attacking him. Poor old

Crush got smacked right in the hooter and dropped into the footwell of the passenger seat, his eyes crossed.

Miser wrapped his tentacles around Brian's throat and squeezed like a boa constrictor. Brian's eyes bulged more than ever and his fat tongue popped out of his mouth as if it was trying to wriggle out of his head. He managed to grab a part of Miser's tentacle and bit down on it hard. Miser yelped in pain, but help was on its way from above.

'Bombs away!' shouted Hoot, who proceeded to drop a very dusty but extremely angry Stan on to the front of the truck. This time, when Stan swung his huge red fist back it would complete its journey to the middle of Brian's creepy puffy face.

POW!

You often hear the expression, 'He didn't know what hit him', but it was never truer than in this case. One second Brian was conscious of biting something invisible that was wrapped around his neck, the next he was slumped across the steering wheel completely unconscious.

The monsters jumped free of the truck just as it careered off the road and slammed into a telegraph pole. Brian's big slippery body shot out through the open windscreen, sailed through the air and crashed straight through the tiled roof of a nearby cowshed.

'Stop the car, Jesus,' said Spike, and Jesus pulled the car over on the side of the road. 'Thank you, Jesus,' said Spike, and Jesus replied with a low, dreary moan. 'Huuurgh.'

Nelson was already running across the road to where Crush, Miser and Stan lay coughing and spluttering in the dust.

'Are you all right?' cried Nelson.

'Did we get 'im?' snarled Stan, struggling to his feet, and Nelson turned to the cowshed. Apart from some seriously freaked-out cattle, there was no sign of life.

'We must be sure. Follow me,' hissed Miser.

'Let's just go. He won't come after us again,' suggested Nelson, but the monsters, including Nosh, were already running towards the cowshed.

DON'T DRINK THE WATER

Stan went into the cowshed on his own, clearly hoping to find Brian alive so that he could punch him on the nose again, but after a few silent seconds he called to Nelson, 'Don't worry, it's safe!'

Nelson stepped into the shed, and as his eyes adjusted to the darkness, he saw Brian lying in the middle of a huge pile of hay: the white, bulging fish eyes were gone, and in their place two very sad blue eyes looked up at Nelson.

'I should never have kissed her,' the man whispered. 'For years I have been her slave. But now . . . now I am free,' he croaked, and started to cough.

This wasn't what Nelson had been expecting at all. 'Uh . . . do you want me to get you some water?' he offered, and Brian's eyes became wide with terror.

'No! Don't drink the water!' he wheezed. 'She poisoned the water. The day I put her in there. The water. It turned black. The flowers. They all died.'

'What do you mean?'

'You cannot save your sister,' whispered Brian.

'What? You know where my sister is?' said Nelson with a great gasp, and Brian reached out and grabbed Nelson's

191

wrist with his huge meaty hand.

'Turn back. You must turn back. You're just a boy. If you don't, you'll regret it.'

I may be a boy, thought Nelson, but I'm a boy with seven monsters who's managed to travel all the way to Brazil. And you're the one lying in the straw.

'I'm sorry,' Brian said with the saddest smile Nelson had ever seen. 'It was her kiss. She poisoned me. She made me do it.'

'Who are you talking about?'

'Carla. Your Auntie Carla. My . . . my wife.'

'Who are you?'

'Brian.'

And with one loud exhale that sounded like someone climbing into their own bed after a very long day, Brian closed his eyes and drifted away.

CHOOSE YOUR COW

'I know he tried to kill me, but we can't just leave him there!' protested Nelson as he followed the monsters out of the cowshed.

'Oh, great,' moaned Spike sarcastically. 'We'll just lug a massive unconscious bloke around with us then, shall we? Or better still, we could stand around here discussing it.' Even though Spike's sarcastic tone was deeply irritating, Nelson couldn't help thinking he had a point.

But it was all so confusing.

If Brian was married to Nelson's sort-of Auntie Carla, wouldn't that make him his sort-of uncle? How could he have been Carla's slave if she had died in the fire? And why would he want to ram him off the road?

Spike pointed to the motorway about half a mile away. 'Look at them all, in their perfectly working cars. It's all right for some, isn't it? Never me though.'

'What are you talking about?' asked Nelson, and Spike pointed to liquid pooling out from under the limo. The smell told Nelson it was petrol.

'We must've gone over a rock when we came off the road. It's ripped the tank right open.'

'Great! JUST GREAT! You were supposed to be controllin' the driver!' bellowed Stan.

'I can't make rocks disappear, you stupid angry tomato!' yelled Spike.

Stan squared up to Spike, desperate to punch him in his spiky head, and he would have done had it not been for the police sirens.

Everyone turned to look in the same direction. There wasn't a police car to be seen, but the sirens were getting louder and they all knew it was just a matter of seconds before one came over the horizon.

In that moment of panic, it was Miser who spoke first. 'Master Nelson, there is not a moment to lose. You must choose your cow.'

'Choose my cow?' said Nelson, turning to see Miser pointing at the herd of cattle who were staring at Nelson and his monsters as if glued to a thrilling TV show.

'Indeed. Hoot can fly, so we shall only need seven of the animals. Might I suggest the bull? I think it most appropriate for you, Master Nelson,' said Miser, gesturing towards a hefty-looking fellow at the front of the herd. 'These beasts are strong; they will carry us quickly. With some assistance from Master Spike, we shall make good time.'

'Seven needles?! If I take out seven needles I'll lose all my water and shrivel up,' complained Spike, showing the small hole in his arm that was still leaking from earlier.

'Sorry, just a second,' said Nelson, holding up his hand

as if in class. 'Are you saying that Spike should do that thing with his needles to all those cows so we can ride them?'

'Well, of course, if you have a better plan, Master Nelson?' replied Miser with a slight bow, but Nelson did not, and exactly twenty-six seconds later six cows and the bull stood very still with wide, googly eyes and a cactus needle sticking out of their foreheads while the monsters did their humming thing and pointed the way to Celeste.

Spike was leaking water from the new holes in his green flesh but stood with his straggly arms raised before the herd like the conductor of a cow choir.

'Cows! You will do as I command! You will carry us and you will run as fast as you can, and not stop until we have reached Celeste,' shouted Spike, but cows being a bit on the stupid side of things only heard the words, 'You . . . run . . . not . . . stop . . .' And with a great 'Moooo!' all seven set off at a speed normally reserved for the likes of zebra being chased by lions. This would have been a fantastic start to the next leg of their journey had Nelson and his monsters actually been on the cows' backs at the time.

Seven monsters and one boy instantly gave chase.

'Couldn't you have waited until we were sitting on them?' shouted Nelson.

'It's not my fault! They're stupid cows!' yelled Spike.

'Tell them to stop!' begged Nelson, his fists pumping like pistons.

'Catchy cows! Catchy cows!' shouted Nosh, rolling through the dirt like a runaway bowling ball.

'I say! Shouldn't you chaps be riding these horseys?' called Hoot from above.

'They're cows, yer great berk!' cried Stan, whose little legs were struggling to carry his enormous upper half. The rest of the monsters howled and yelled and screamed and above all ran as fast as they could after the cows.

The herd stampeded down through the field and ran straight into a narrow river. The splash was immense and the water deep, but that didn't stop them from swimming towards the other side. Luckily cows aren't very fast swimmers.

'This is our chance! Jump on!' cried Nelson, launching himself off the riverbank. The water that engulfed him was so cold that Nelson would have screamed but his lungs seemed to have shrunk to the size of two Brussels sprouts. All around, the river was erupting as the monsters landed like bombs among the herd.

'It looks very cold,' said Spike, hesitating at the river's edge before Stan sent him sailing through the air and into the water with a great kick in the backside, before leaping in himself.

Nelson reached out, grabbed the tail of the bull and pulled himself forward. Only now did he realize just how huge the bull was. Its back was easily as wide as a kitchen table, and his huge white horns were as long as Nelson's own arms! Though they were clearly to be avoided under normal circumstances, the horns gave Nelson something to grab on to, and with a great heave he managed to swing his right leg over the bull's back. As he looked around he saw his monsters clawing and pulling their way on to the backs of the herd too.

'Bravo!' shouted Hoot from above, but none of them could hear for the great crashing of water and the pounding of hoofs as the cows arrived on the other side of the river and thundered up the bank.

Jesus sat in his petrol-drained limo feeling incredibly envious of all the other cars zooming along the highway. Spike had made sure he had a clear memory of driving to the airport in order to pick up his client Donna Gatsky, only to be rammed off the road on his way there by a crazy truck driver who was now lying unconscious in the cowshed. Not only would the police completely believe Jesus, they would ask for his autograph as several officers had been his biggest fans when he had been a kick-boxer.

As for the man lying in the cowshed . . . the police would discover he was extremely concussed and recovering from ten years of deep hypnosis. They would have to investigate his story further . . .

ABBA'S GREATEST HITS

'Waterloo' by ABBA blasted from a speaker in Uncle Pogo's false leg. ABBA was the first artist on Pogo's alphabetical playlist, and since it had been triggered by all the bouncing around of Nelson's backpack, ABBA's greatest hits would now provide the soundtrack to their stampede across the dusty orange plains towards the dark green strip of jungle on the horizon.

Above them Hoot sailed through the sky with enviable ease, the Brazilian sun glinting off his golden feathers.

With his left hand gripping the bull's coat as tightly as possible, Nelson reached up with his right and grasped the pendant that bounced against his chest. A howl came out of him as if from nowhere.

Not a scary or sad howl, but a loud and happy howl. A sound that said to the world, 'I AM GOING TO SAVE MY SISTER!' And apart from Spike, who was feeling weak from all the water leaking out of him, the rest of the monsters howled too. Even the cows joined in with the happy feeling and mooed for all they were worth. By the time ABBA had got around to singing 'SOS', Nelson and his monsters had reached the edge of the jungle and the only light left in the sky was the ever-darkening remnants of a pink and gold sunset.

HOT-DOG MISSILES

'I'm too weak. I can't control the cows any more,' said Spike, but he spoke in barely a whisper and Nelson didn't hear him.

He didn't need to; one look at the cactus monster barely clinging to the back of a rampaging cow told Nelson everything he needed to know. Spike's skin was no longer bright green and rubbery. It was a dull brown and shrivelled and bits of it were peeling off. For the first time ever, Spike had every reason to moan.

'He's leaked too much! He needs water!' shouted Nelson to Puff, but Puff just yawned and continued to cling on to his cow like a great purple blanket spread across its back. Nelson turned to Miser on his left side and shouted, 'Spike needs water! We need to stop!' At that very same moment, the bull Nelson was riding charged straight through a large bush, which was shredded by its horns, covering Nelson in splinters.

'If we stop now we shall lose the herd, Master Nelson!' said Miser, using his tentacles like whips to spur on his cow.

'But what about Spike?'

'Who cares about that moaner?! We have to get to Celeste!' bellowed Stan.

'Nelly-son! Nelly-son! We almost there! We almost there! Nosh feel it in his big belly!' cried Nosh, who proceeded to blast flames out of the top of his head after digesting a delicious branch that had snapped off in his cobblestone teeth only a few moments before.

'Hold on, Spike! We're not far now!' called Nelson, but at that very moment Spike's cow jumped a fallen tree and Spike lost his grip, tumbling from the back of the cow and rolling in the dirt.

'SPIKE!' shouted Nelson, and let go of his bull, but his ankles were so unprepared for the landing that they twisted beneath him.

SKRONCH!

Nelson rose from the dust, coughing and spitting out bits of twig as he ran towards the spot where Spike lay.

The rest of the monsters realized Nelson's change of direction and reluctantly leaped from their cows, who ignored the fact their passengers had disembarked and continued to charge through the jungle at high speed.

Nelson cradled the brown husk that was Spike without fear of being pricked by needles as they had all fallen out now.

'Spike? Spike?' he said, panting furiously.

'Water,' whispered Spike through parched lips.

Nelson looked around in a panic.

'Hoot! See if you can find some water. Even a tiny bit.

There must be some nearby.'

'Water? Splendid idea! I am rather thirsty.'

'Not for you, for Spike!' yelled Nelson.

'Ah! Yes, I must say he does look rather dehydrated.' Hoot took off through the trees.

The sound of the stampeding cattle receded into the distance, making room for the chirrup of crickets and the chatter of parrots to be heard instead.

'What's . . . the . . . problem? He'll . . . be fine,' drawled Puff.

'He's not fine though, is he? I mean, look at him,' said Nelson, looking down into Spike's now hollow eyes.

''E'll bounce back. 'E's a cactus, innit?' Stan stomped angrily on a branch, snapping it in two.

'Master Nelson, there are times when one must make sacrifices for the greater good,' said Miser, bowing low to avoid Nelson's gaze.

'Sacrifice Spike? Just leave him behind in the dust? All he needs is water. Then we can carry on.' Nelson addressed the entire group, as it was clear they were all on Miser's side.

The awkward silence was broken by a very loud call from Hoot, who sailed through the trees towards them.

'Fear not, my dears! Once again, good ol' Hoot has come up trumps and saved the day! With my keen eye I have spied us some water, here beneath these rocks no less. But please, there is no need to shower me with praise. I already know how much you admire me and I can't blame you – I am rather dazzling, aren't it? Now follow me, it's just over here. Step lively. Come on now. Look sharp.'

'Gawd, I hate that bird,' growled Stan.

Nelson carried Spike in his arms (which was very easy as, without water, Spike was feather-light) to where the rest of the monsters stood gazing into a gap between two huge bare orange boulders.

'Clever old me tossed a stone down there and heard a plop. All the water you need!' announced Hoot.

Looking down, Nelson only saw darkness and heard the echo of Hoot's words.

'Are you sure?' he asked, as the ends of Spike's arms began to crack and wither into dust.

Hoot tossed a pebble into the hole.

There was a pause.

A long pause.

And then finally a plop. A distant but significant plop.

'Hoot, it's flippin' miles down there!' exclaimed Nelson.

'I do jump-jump!' said Nosh, bouncing up and down like an excited sack of potatoes, and before Nelson could tell him that was a bad idea, Nosh had slid down between the rocks with a great 'Wheeeeeeeeeee!'

'Nosh! No!' cried Nelson, but it was too late. Nosh had gone, his voice tailing off into the distance like the whistle of a cartoon anvil about to fall on someone's head.

Then silence. Nelson and the remaining monsters held their breath.

SPLASH!

It might have been a mile away, but it was definitely a splash.

'Nosh? Nosh? Are you OK?' called Nelson, but Nosh didn't reply, he was too busy laughing.

'Jumpy-jumpy!' he cried, clearly having a whale of a time.

'Hoot. Fly down there and bring up some water in your beak or something. Fast as you can – I think Spike's stopped breathing.'

'Ah, now, there's the hitch, sir. I'm afraid I cannot fly into this cave for it is dark and a tad on the scary side.'

You couldn't hear Nelson begging Hoot to reconsider over the sound of the other monsters cursing Hoot at the top of their lungs.

'HONK!' blasted Crush, sending Hoot flying up into the trees.

'Can one of you take Spike?' begged Nelson, but it was clear from all their faces that this was not going to happen without an awful lot of wasted time.

Nelson was going to have to jump with Spike by himself. He'd never even had the guts to jump off the top board at the swimming pool before, but because he was cradling a monster that needed water to survive, he had no choice.

He might well be scared.

He might even scream.

But he HAD to jump.

And he did.

Well, he didn't jump at first. He sort of skidded down the rocks until his trainers couldn't keep up, and just when he felt he was going to fall on his face again, he jumped. And he screamed. All the way down through the inky blackness. Falling and falling and falling through the air and finally crashing with an explosive POW into the waters below.

Seconds later there were bomb-sized splashes all around him as the other monsters landed in the water.

Nelson sank so deeply into the pool that it took him several seconds before he could kick to the surface again with Spike in his arms.

As he broke the surface, Nelson instinctively flicked his head so that his fringe flew out of his eyes. He didn't need to swim to the rocks at the side of the pool because Miser was already on a dry rock and reached out a tentacle to pull him in with great ease. Everyone was laughing at the thrill of it all, and when Nelson realized he could stand as he raised Spike from the water, he found the patient looking back at him with a stunned but reassuringly lively expression.

They had landed in a cave of indeterminate size, as the only light came from the gap between the two boulders above.

'Ooh, look at the little baby!' said Stan, who was watching Spike gurgle and blink himself back to life in Nelson's arms. The monsters' laughter echoed around the dark cave, which gave Nelson a fleeting memory of standing beneath the dark dome of St Paul's Cathedral the night he had made his monsters.

'I say! Not so bad after all, eh?' called Hoot as he spiralled down towards the others, but they were all too happy to bother throwing a rock at his head.

'Ow!' said Nelson, as cactus needles began to protrude once again from Spike's rubbery flesh. Crush ran to Nelson's side and hugged him with all his might (which was a great deal of might).

'Honk!'

Spike sat up by himself and blinked slowly as he twisted his body back to life. 'What are we doing down here? What happened to the cows?' he said.

BANG!

The noise was so loud it was minutes before anyone would hear anything other than the ringing in their ears. The explosion had been magnified in volume by the cave acting as an echo chamber. The blast of air that accompanied the noise sent every single one of them flying back into the water, and when they finally rose to the surface, terrified out of their wits, they found the air to be full of swirling blue smoke.

At this precise point in time, just outside St Paul's Cathedral, a young man called Frank Mole was serving hot dogs from his small kiosk to a couple of football supporters on their way to a match.

BANG!

The explosion happened right beside Frank's kiosk and sent hot dogs flying in all directions. No one was hurt, but for few terrifying seconds Frank Mole thought he was covered in blood, until he realized it was actually his own tomato ketchup. As a cloud of blue smoke drifted away on the breeze people turned to see the patch of scorched earth where the explosion had taken place.

What they couldn't see was a very, very startled monster standing in the middle of it all. It was Nosh, and he was as surprised to be there as the folks who were picking themselves off the floor. And the reason for his sudden appearance was about to pop out of his mouth.

Nosh had never once eaten anything he found disagreeable, and this was the first time he had ever thrown up. The Bang Stone fell out of his mouth and on to the pavement, where it fizzed for a moment before Nosh quickly picked it up again and stuffed it back into his mouth.

BANG!

The poor people who had already been scared senseless by the first explosion screamed for their lives at the second blast, and Frank Mole decided that although he had found this spot to be extremely profitable over the years, from now on he would sell his hot dogs somewhere else.

BANG!

Just as Nelson and the monsters had begun to haul themselves out of the water, yet another explosion sent them flying backwards.

This time, when the blue smoke cleared, they would find the culprit of this loud and very, very scary incident.

Nosh threw up the stone and this time he put it back where he had found it: inside the little clay pot that he'd discovered in the bag Miser had secretly stolen from Brian. Nosh would never have gone looking through

Miser's belongings, or anyone else's for that matter, but the stench of rotten eggs was irresistible, and he was *so* hungry. It was this eggy smell that had reminded him of one of the other smells he liked the most, which was fried onions. He had caught a whiff of them from a hot-dog stand beside the tube-station entrance when he and the monsters had escaped from St Paul's Cathedral and begun their journey to find Nelson, and it was precisely this place he had been thinking of when he popped the strange eggy stone in his mouth and exploded.

'What on earth did you just do, Nosh?' spluttered Nelson, as he collapsed on the rock for the second time.

'I explode,' said Nosh, shuffling his feet awkwardly as if about to be told off.

'Yeah, I know that, but how come you're still alive?' said Nelson.

'Hot dogs,' said Nosh. 'Nosh fink of hot dogs and Nosh go bang! And me go to da hot-dog man,' said Nosh, rubbing his empty belly, wishing that he'd picked up a few of those stray frankfurters.

'What hot-dog man? Where?' said Nelson.

'Da big church. Where Nelly-son make us.'

'St Paul's Cathedral?' said Nelson. This made no sense.

'Yeah! San Pauly Thedral! Yeah! I eat stone, I fink of hot-dog place by Pauly Thedral and BANG! I there. Then I fink, oh no, I wanna be back wiv Nelly-son, so I eat eggy stone and I fink of Nelly-son, and BANG! I back to Nelly-son!'

Nelson could have berated Miser for stealing Brian's belongings or Nosh for letting his hunger win out over common sense, but there was no doubt that without Miser's greed or Nosh's gluttony they would never have discovered the Bang Stone. This must be that magic stone his uncle had told him about. The one that had enabled Pogo's dad to travel to Brazil and back so quickly. With this stone they could travel directly to Celeste without another wasted moment. It was a gift beyond value.

'This actually might explain things a bit,' said Nelson. 'On the news they said there'd been an explosion on the boat my sister was on. It could have been the same as this. Yeah, Brian must have eaten one of those stones. He must have swallowed it and taken my sister with him.'

Nosh had agreed to swallow the stone again and was already looking forward to having the eggy taste back in his mouth. The rest of the gang huddled around him, reluctantly preparing to give Nosh a big hug.

Hoot cleared his throat and spoke loudly and clearly to the group. 'Now then, just in case we are all blown to smithereens, I would just like to say how much I have enjoyed your company as I am quite sure you have enjoyed mine. And if by some astonishing miracle we should survive this explosion, I would like to offer each of you my very own styling and grooming tips, which I guarantee will vastly improve the looks of even the most hideous of you. Very good. Carry on.'

The rest of the monsters were too stunned by his arrogance to reply.

'OK, is everyone ready?' said Nelson.

'HONK! HONK! HOOONK!' said Crush.

Nelson held hands with Miser and Stan. Puff had crawled up on to Nosh's head like an ill-fitting purple wig, and Crush wrapped his arms around Nelson's neck and clung on.

'Why do I have to hold hands with Hoot? He's a total berk,' said Spike, but no one took any notice. Miser took Spike's other hand and they all squeezed in around Nosh.

'You ready, Nelly-son?' asked Nosh, as he opened the clay pot and the stench of sulphur shot up their noses like a stinky bullet.

'We just close our eyes, we think of her and we say her name – OK?' said Nelson, and all the monsters nodded. 'Right. Phew. This is it. If this works, we're gonna rescue my sister. OK, do it, Nosh.'

Nosh greedily stuffed the blue stone into his mouth.

Nelson and the seven monsters closed their eyes, pulled each other close and said, 'Celeste.'

THE JELLY FREAKS

Nelson didn't feel anything. He didn't even hear a bang. But when he opened his eyes he and his seven monsters were enveloped by a thick, swirling blue smoke which rushed into his lungs, causing him to cough so hard Crush fell from his neck.

'I say, did that actually work? Are we there?' spluttered Hoot. There was no way of knowing where they were – the smoke was too thick – but it didn't sound as if they were in the cave any more.

Nosh gagged and threw his arms out to push everybody back. Plop. Fizz. The stone fell out of his mouth and shook urgently on the ground like a beetle stuck on its back. Miser whipped up the stone in a flash and sealed it inside Brian's clay pot, where you could still hear it trembling as if it wanted to get out. Still no one said anything. Their eyes were wide as they scanned for any sign of where they were. One thing was for sure: it was a hundred times hotter here than it had been in that cold cave. It even sounded as if the world around them was sizzling like sausages in a frying pan.

Nelson pulled his T-shirt over his mouth, turned

around and slowly raised a hand through the smoke. He'd not reached more than a few centimetres when his fingers discovered the unmistakable ridges of tree bark. Nelson wondered how anything so close to him could be hidden from sight. He leaned forward to see what his hand had found – and a terrifying face loomed through the blue smoke, frozen in a silent scream.

Nelson jumped back, bracing himself as if whatever he had touched would come for him.

But it didn't.

'Master Nelson,' whispered Miser, 'what have you seen?'

Spike answered for him.

'A bunch of boring trees. Look.' He pointed upward, and through the swirling smoke they could all clearly make out the silhouettes of trees.

Nelson looked back to the place where he had seen the horrible face and saw it was nothing more than the knot of a tree trunk. His mind had played a trick on him. But the tree was black as if someone had painted it with a layer of tar. Nelson looked down at his hand. His fingers were covered in something oily and black.

Crush let out the tiniest of honks. Actually, it was more like the sound of a puppy cowering in the kitchen on fireworks night. That one nervous, trembling note summed up just how they all felt at that moment.

The smoke began to drift away, like ghosts who had had

enough of haunting for one night and were going back to bed.

As the world around them started to appear, Nelson clung to his pendant. The good feeling it provided had never felt more necessary.

Nelson and his seven monsters were standing in the middle of a scorched patch of jungle. The trees around them were baked black and leaned so far out from the clearing it was a miracle they hadn't toppled over.

'Briii-aaan,' came a haunting female voice through the trees.

'CELESTE!' screamed Nelson, setting off at full speed in the direction of the voice.

The monsters gave chase, roaring and hissing and shouting and honking as loudly as they could.

Running was not easy. The jungle floor was a web of wet and rubbery vines covered in a layer of black oil and Nelson's trainers might as well have been greased with butter the way they slid out from under him at every step and sent him crashing to his knees. The monsters fared no better.

Nelson stopped. In the short distance he had travelled, he had already managed to completely lose his sense of direction. Looking back, he couldn't even see the patch of scorched earth any more. This had to be the very worst rescue of all time.

Flop . . . Flop . . . Flop . . .

Nelson turned his head towards the sound of something

or somethings landing repeatedly on the wet ground nearby. He held up his hand to the monsters behind him, ordering them to stop. And surprisingly, they did as they were told.

Flop . . . Flop . . . Flop . . .

This time the monsters heard it too.

Nelson proceeded cautiously and the monsters followed suit. As they slid past an impossibly large and equally sticky black tree trunk, Nelson and his monsters were greeted by a very strange sight indeed.

From a pond filled to the brim with disgusting-looking black water, lots of strange and extremely ugly little fish were leaping on to the mud. As the black water dripped off them Nelson saw that they had jellified bodies and huge white eyes that bulged from their heads with an eerie, soulless stare that matched Brian's.

'Don't drink the water,' whispered Nelson, remembering Brian's final words.

Flop . . . Flop . . . Flop . . .

More horrid little fish joined the slippery pile that now lay gasping for air.

'Jellyfishes! Me eat one, please?' begged Nosh, who was drooling like crazy, but the others ignored him.

'We have to find Celeste!' said Nelson with rising panic.

'Then we must close our eyes and say her name,' whispered Miser, and the monsters settled into their usual trance.

'Celeste,' they chanted, and stood very still and did the pointing thing.

Nelson turned to see that they were all pointing directly at the pool of black water.

'That can't be right. Celeste!' shouted Nelson, turning in order to broadcast his voice as far and as wide as possible.

'Spread out! Everyone spread out!' shouted Stan.

'Celeste! Where are you?' cried Nelson, and he felt Crush tugging at his leg. 'Not now, Crush!'

Crush honked like a car stuck in traffic.

'What?' snapped Nelson, looking down with an angry glare. Crush cowered.

'Stop it! I wasn't going to hit you, you silly thing. What do you want?'

Crush pointed to the spot where the ugly little fish had landed.

Except that they weren't ugly or little any more. Or even fish.

217

In just a few seconds their jellified bodies had evolved into something far uglier and scarier, no longer gasping for breath, but breathing quickly and easily. Legs and claws had replaced the useless fins. And the ghastly creatures were already double their original size and growing by the second. Remember, the first creatures on Planet Earth had evolved from this very pool of water – and still did. But a process that used to take millions of years now happened within a few seconds. Had the water been pure like it used to be, these fish might have evolved into rather nice humans, but now the water was polluted by Carla's hatred and the creatures squirmed and shrieked as their skins stretched like inflating balloons, new bones grew like splinters in their new limbs and new joints popped and snapped into place.

'Jelly freaks!' shouted Nosh, who decided he didn't want to eat them any more but would rather run away from them as quickly as possible.

'Nosh must have made a mistake in bringing us here. I suggest we leave quickly, Master Nelson. There is no sign of Celeste,' said Miser, as he and the other monsters backed away from the evolving fish creatures.

Nelson's mind whizzed. Where on earth were they? If they all thought of Celeste when they used the Bang Stone, then why wasn't she here?

Nelson grasped the pendant, closed his eyes and tried to

bat all of the doubts and fears out of his head.

'CELESTE!' he yelled, his voice was much, much louder than it had ever been before. It echoed through the thick jungle with all the power of a lion's roar.

The monsters joined in. 'CELESTE!' they screamed in unison, and they would have continued, had it not been for another tug and warning honk from Crush.

'HONK! HONK! HONK!'

Nelson and the other monsters turned to discover something terrifying: what only moments ago had been ugly little fish sprouting limbs were now as large as dogs and heading straight for them.

Until now I have assumed you could sort of imagine what these evolving creatures looked like, but just before things turn very nasty indeed, here is a picture of how the fish had changed into what was about to make our heroes run for their lives.

Remember, this is just a rough drawing. Not even the greatest artist in the world could capture just how terrifying these things really were.

'RUN!' shouted Nelson. But most of the monsters were already running as fast as they could. Even Puff was tearing through that jungle, fuelled by a rocket tank's worth of fear, as fast as his fat paws would carry him.

Nosh tore through bushes and bounced over roots and vines in his bowling-ball mode, his pink body almost completely covered in the black goo. He had no idea where he was going and neither did any of the others.

The only thing they were worried about now was staying ahead of those horrible creatures. None of them turned around to look again, which was a good thing, because their pursuers had doubled in size again.

You would have thought Hoot would have a huge advantage in being able to fly, but remember that he is also spectacularly stupid, and he had managed to slam straight into a branch. His beak made a sound like a church bell striking one o'clock, before he fell to the ground right in front of Nelson. Nelson tripped over him and threw his arms out to brace himself for the inevitable fall, but before his hands hit the ground he felt himself being yanked backwards as if on a bungee cord.

The sound of the monsters screaming and running for their lives was suddenly muted, and the world around Nelson became blurry. He was upside down and felt as if he was being squeezed on all sides like a supermarket chicken breast trapped under cling film. It took him at least twelve seconds to realize he had been eaten whole for the second time in twenty-four hours!

He was inside the belly of one of those awful creatures who had been chasing them through the jungle. The creature's guts grumbled around Nelson and he felt the belly he was in swinging from side to side. The mutant was moving, and as it did, it grew: its ghastly, throbbing veins threading their way through its ever-expanding jellified flesh like red worms.

It wasn't just Nelson who had become a snack. All of

his monsters were now squirming inside the bellies of these terrible creatures, who were heading back to the pool they had sprung from as fish less than a minute before.

The air inside this creature was running out and it wouldn't be long before Nelson would turn blue and pass out. His heart thumped so hard in his chest he could feel it beating in every part of his body. It was precisely at this moment that the creature's stomach contracted sharply and Nelson suddenly shot up and out of its mouth, before tumbling through the air and landing with a loud slap in the black mud surrounding the pool.

Seven more slaps followed, and Nelson saw his seven monsters being blasted from the mouths of the hideous jelly freaks. Crush was the first to get to his feet. He came and hugged Nelson as the other six slopped through the mud to cluster around him. Nelson could tell the monsters were as frightened as he was.

'One ... two ... three ... four ... five ... six ... seven ...' said a ghostly female voice, and Nelson whipped around to see a gigantic whale-like face staring at him.

'Seven little monsters and one little boy,' said the whale thing, its mouth so huge that it took her twice as long to say things as it would you or me. 'I'm sorry my little friends had to eat you in order to bring you here to me.'

'H-how come it can see you guys?' whispered Nelson.

His monsters shrugged. 'It takes one . . . to know one?' suggested Puff, in barely a whisper.

'But where is my beloved Brian?' said the whale thing, its eyes peering into the trees behind them.

'Ah. I think she means that awfully large fellow who was out cold in the cowshed?' said Hoot in a cheerful voice, as if he'd guessed the answer in a jolly quiz game. It was too late to punch him to shut him up, but Stan did it anyway. Whack!

'Ouchy!'

'Shut it, bird brain,' whispered Stan angrily.

'You mean my husband is . . . dead?' asked the whale, as it placed two of its rubbery fins in the mud surrounding the pool.

Nelson instinctively backed away, his bottom sliding through the mud as he pushed with his heels and his elbows. Brian was her husband? This couldn't be his Auntie Carla . . . could it?

Stan was squaring up to the creature. 'Who knows? Anyway, it was 'is own fault! The stupid bloke tried to smash us off the road!' Stan was trying to sound like his usual tough self but not doing a very good job of it.

Crush let out a low honk, though not in fear of Carla. The jelly freaks were beginning to grow their first set of teeth. And judging by the growls and howls coming from the pack, growing teeth this fast was an extremely painful process.

'Oh, my poor Brian,' said the whale, closing its eyes

and taking a deep breath. Nelson could feel the air around him being sucked into that huge mouth before it let out a loud and extremely smelly sigh.

'At least he did what I wanted,' said the whale, looking Nelson straight in the eye. 'I asked him to find you, and here you are.'

'Where's my sister?' said Nelson, in a voice that was much louder than he had been aiming for. It was the voice of someone who was not to be trifled with.

'You must love her to have come all this way to save her.'

'She's my sister.'

'Yes, and I will give her back to you very shortly.'

Nelson and the monsters all felt the same shot of hope hit them square in the chest.

The whale thing continued: 'But first you must give something to me.'

Nelson didn't hesitate. 'Anything. What do you want?'

'Only that pendant I see you have around your neck.'

'Why?'

'It belonged . . . to *my* sister,' said the whale. It's hard to tell if a water creature is crying, but it definitely looked as if it was getting a bit emotional.

'It's your *sister's*? Wait – does that mean . . . you *are* my Auntie Carla?' said Nelson, finally putting the pieces of that blasted jigsaw together.

Carla nodded and batted her eyelids.

Nelson put his hand to his chest and felt the pendant.

A remnant of the story Uncle Pogo had told him flashed into his mind: the father who poured all of his love into a stone in order to save his dying daughter. Nelson had thought his uncle was making it up, but the world was very different to how it had been only a few days ago. Now it was place where magic could happen, where monsters really did exist. And therefore, a place where a father really could save his dying daughter by pouring every single drop of love he had in his heart into a stone.

Carla, this hideous creature, the twin that survived, wanted her father's love in return for Nelson's sister. It seemed like a good deal. He would miss the waves of hope and peacefulness the pendant gave him in times of need, but he could live without those. What he couldn't live without was his sister. Nelson reached into the neck of his T-shirt and pulled out the pendant.

PARADISE

Nelson gripped the pendant and raised it above his head so that the chain swung away from his neck.

Carla's great eyes grew bigger.

'Master Nelson,' hissed Miser, 'might I suggest you hold on to that item of jewellery until we have seen Celeste for ourselves?'

Carla had heard.

'I promise you will have her back, just as soon as you give me that pendant,' she said in her slow, dreamy tone.

With the pendant dangling from his right hand, Nelson raised himself to his feet.

Though Carla was huge and ugly, as he approached Nelson could see the very real glimmer of hope in her bulging eyes.

With every one of the six, squelchy steps Nelson took towards her, Carla opened her great mouth wider and wider, so that by the time he was standing no more than a few centimetres from the edge of the pond, her mouth gaped as wide open as the boot of a saloon car.

Nelson looked at his monsters, and all seven of them looked back at him with a mixture of fear and confusion.

The pendant swung on the end of its chain, drawn forward by Carla taking a great breath.

'Wait,' said Nelson, and Carla glared. 'When you took the pendant from Isabelle, you got burned. If I give it to you, you'll just get burned again.'

Carla blinked. 'Not this time. This time I am ready. I shall be born again.'

Nelson looked into Carla's great mouth, and without another thought dropped the pendant in as if she was a wishing well.

As the very last link of the chain left his fingers, Nelson suddenly felt all hope was lost. He tried to grab it back, but it was too late.

Snap!

Carla's mouth slammed shut and she sank like a

submarine into the bubbling black water. Gone.

The jelly freaks snarled and ground their teeth and Nelson's monsters jumped to their feet and ran to his side.

'Gah! She tricked us. The witch has tricked us!' hissed Miser.

Spike burst into tears and the others were too shocked to speak.

'Celeste!' yelled Nelson, turning to face the black trees in case she was being held somewhere among them. 'Celeste!'

As if in answer to his call, a fresh green shoot suddenly popped up out of the mud between his shoes. Pop. Another one right beside it. Pop. And another.

The mud around the pond began to bubble, and luscious green shoots sprouted everywhere before blossoming into magnificent flowers.

'What's going on?' cried Nelson, as he was knocked off his feet by an entire bouquet of yellow flowers pushing their way up through the ground. The oily mud churned, turning back to its original rich rust-brown clay. The bark of scorched tree trunks fell away like scabs to reveal fresh healthy bark beneath. A million luscious green leaves fanned out like magicians' cards from a hundred thousand branches that were twisting and turning up towards the rays of sun breaking through the jungle canopy for the first time in ten long, dark years.

The jelly freaks continued to swell and sprout new

features while their bulging white eyes remained empty of any emotion, but they didn't look as if they were about to attack any more.

Nelson felt as if he was watching a nightmare turn into a dream. Above him, the buds of magnolia trees were opening so quickly that the blossom exploded in snowy clouds of pink petals. Colour and life consumed all that had been black and dead with the scale and spectacle of an Olympic opening ceremony.

Nelson felt his shoes fill with water and spun around to see the pond overflowing. The black water belched out of the ground before bulging as Carla broke the oily black surface once again. This time her entire body launched out of the pond, like a killer whale in a sea-park display, scattering Nelson and the monsters, who fled just in time to avoid being crushed. Carla's phenomenal blubbery bulk slammed on to flowers and grasses and bushes and plants that were clamouring for their place in the sun. The tremor of her landing knocked everything, including several nice new trees, to the ground.

Behind her, the pond that had been as black as an inkwell, now overflowed with sparkling spring water and slowly began to shrink, its grassy banks drawing tighter and tighter as if to close completely.

Suddenly Carla gave a great belch, opened her huge mouth and Celeste slid down Carla's fat purple tongue and into a bed of spiralling orchids.

Nosh, Spike, Puff, Miser, Hoot, Stan and Nelson all cried her name in unison.

'Celeste!'

(Crush honked, of course.)

Nelson ran through the swaying grasses towards his sister, skidding to his knees at her side and cradling her sleeping head in his arms. Her blonde hair was black now, and her skin as white as the moon, but these were utterly insignificant details compared to the gigantic and wonderful fact that Nelson had found his sister at last.

The monsters pushed and shoved like paparazzi trying to get near a movie star, knocking Nelson over.

'Hey, watch it,' Nelson laughed, but the monsters were desperate to be as close to Celeste as possible, as if the ache that they had been cursed with since they were created would finally be cured.

It was the happiest day the jungle had ever known in its entire billion-year history.

But as warmth and colour saturated the world around him, a rush of ice-cold horror ran through Nelson's veins. His big sister was not asleep in his arms.

She was dead.

THE DEADLY SEVEN

Laughter rang out through the jungle. It was Carla, her heart filled with a joy she had never known – her father's love.

Nelson knelt by his big sister, a great surge of grief rising in his belly like lava and bursting out of him in a savage howl. And all of Nelson's monsters were howling and screeching with him, for they shared his pain right down to the very marrow in their bones.

Nelson screamed and raged and howled until all the misery and confusion and pain he felt was boiled into just one simple emotion: pure hatred.

Nelson's monsters felt it too. The hatred was so powerful it made them bigger and stronger.

'DESTROY HER!' screamed Stan, his eyes now large and red, already charging towards the gelatinous creature that was Auntie Carla, but he was blocked by one of her jelly freaks smashing a fist into his face and sending him reeling backwards.

Auntie Carla laughed as if she'd just heard the most wonderful joke, while her body started to evolve back into human form.

'It worked! The pendant worked! I am saved!' she cried.

Her laughter only fuelled Stan's hatred, and as he rolled from the blow he grew and grew and grew.

Nelson felt something hit him hard in the back and he fell forward on to the grass. Looking up, he saw Crush towering above him, as tall as an oak tree. His usual honk was replaced with an ear-splitting roar and his mouth was now lined with razor-sharp teeth. Those little arms that used to cling lovingly to Nelson's legs were now as long and as thick as anchor chains, and Crush beat them against the ground, over and over again.

All the monsters were growing larger and more powerful – and they were completely out of control.

Hoot's red eyes became wide and manic, while his beak twisted as he screeched and clawed at the ground beside Nelson.

'Watch out!' screamed Nelson, but Hoot never heard him over all the screeching.

Nelson pulled Celeste out of the way just in time to avoid being squashed by Nosh who had swollen to the size of a bouncy castle and was rolling forward to join Stan.

Stan was now six metres tall, with fists the size of wrecking balls and horns as long as elephant tusks.

One by one the monsters gathered together to face Carla and her jelly freaks. Puff had only grown a little taller but had stretched massively lengthways, like a hairy purple serpent. Those huge eyes that had been closed for most of the time were wide open and burning red. Spike had become gigantic and bristled with needles as long as spears. Miser had grown huge, with even more tentacles thrashing from his barnacled green body as if they had a mind of their own.

Everything he had stolen on his journey was falling out from the pockets in his flesh: medals, coins, jewellery, wallets, keys . . . hundreds of stolen objects poured out of him and fell into the grass.

They were no longer just seven little monsters. They were huge. They were angry. And most of all, they were deadly.

'DESTROY!' roared Stan, and the deadly seven charged towards Carla.

They may have been bigger than the ghastly jelly freaks, but the deadly seven were outnumbered. The two armies clashed in the middle of the prettiest battlefield in the world. Fists pounded monster flesh, razor teeth snapped, claws slashed, hoofs kicked and the ground shook like an earthquake was happening.

Crush and Miser gripped several jelly freaks at once,

allowing Stan to knock them silly with his hammer-blow punches. A jelly freak leaped on to Hoot's back and tried to topple him, but Hoot pinned the creature to the ground with one of his enormous claws and yanked at its rubbery arm as if he was trying to extract a gigantic earthworm from the ground. Spike swung one of his arms and it slammed into the belly of a jelly freak – sending the creature flying backwards into Nosh's wide-open mouth. Nosh swallowed it in two, huge gulps.

'JELLY!' he roared, before his head erupted in a crown of flames – setting fire to the branches in the trees above.

The flames tore across the jungle canopy and showers of sparks rained down.

Nelson cowered over Celeste's lifeless body until the sparks had passed. When he opened his eyes again, the ground around him was peppered with tiny fires.

And that's when Nelson saw Carla.

The monsters were all so busy fighting, none of the deadly seven noticed Carla crawling further and further away. Though her flesh was still translucent, she now had stumpy little arms and legs. Her face was deflating towards a human shape.

Nelson was running towards her, so fast it was as if he had miraculously been turbo-charged, before he knew what he was doing.

WHACK!

Nelson flew backwards through the air before he hit the ground hard. The breath was knocked right out of him, but he managed to roll to the left just in time to avoid a second blow from a jelly freak. None of Nelson's monsters noticed he was in trouble.

For the first time since the monsters had arrived in his life, Nelson felt as if he was on his own.

'MORE JELLY!' roared Nosh and another crown of flames ignited from his head with the roar of a hot-air balloon.

As Nelson scrambled to his feet, burning branches fell around him. The jelly freak who had singled him out picked up one of the largest and the flesh of its hands sizzled like steaks in a frying pan, but still the jelly freak raised the flaming branch above its big head, smoke billowing from his sizzling hands, and it roared, which in jelly-freak speak probably means, 'I AM GOING TO CRUSH YOU!' It might have managed it if it hadn't been for the storm-like rumble preceding the extraordinarily well-timed arrival of the cows.

Yes, the cows.

The very same ones who had been told not under any circumstances to stop until they reached a girl called Celeste, had finally arrived at their destination. And having not let anything get in their way, not even the traffic on a very busy highway, the bull at the head of the herd slammed into the jelly freak about to strike Nelson, sending it flying through the air, where it was caught by Stan, who pulverized it by slamming his two massive fists into either side of its jelly head at the same time.

Nelson stared open-mouthed as the cows continued to run towards the spot where his sister lay, surrounded her and then proceeded to feast on the fresh grass as if it was perfectly normal to graze right next to a giant monster fight.

Carla's new arms and legs might still have had a way to go before they looked like they used to, but that didn't stop her from dancing and singing. She was as full of love and joy as Nelson was of rage and sadness. The pendant had dissolved inside her and released her father's unconditional love into every part of her being. I hope you know what a wonderful feeling it is, to be loved. Having been weighed down by heavy feelings like envy and greed for almost her entire life, Auntie Carla now felt light as a feather and giddy as the winner of a TV game show. She even reached down to pick a flower that had touched her new happy heart with its beauty. It was while she was giving it a sniff with the nose that had started to form on her face that Nelson ran into the back of her with so much force that they both fell forward and tumbled through the swaying grasses. Auntie Carla merely laughed, which just made Nelson even angrier.

He got to his feet and would have charged again had he not been knocked flying by a jelly freak who had been tossed from the battle by Miser.

Nelson and his Auntie Carla fell into the ever-shrinking pond with an almighty splash. Suddenly everything was cold, quiet and suffocating. Nelson was underwater and struggling to swim out from under his aunt's flailing body, but it was Carla who broke the surface first. She gasped before roaring with laughter.

'What fun this is!' she cried.

Nelson was starting to feel the terrifying thump of his heart in his chest as his body screamed for air. He needed to get to the surface, but the way was blocked by Carla's great bulk. And the hole was getting smaller, squeezing her gelatinous body tighter and tighter.

'Ooh! Goodness me! I'm well and truly stuck!' exclaimed Carla. She pushed her hands down in the mud with all her might and heaved her great body upward. Her large tummy flopped up on to the bank.

The hole was now only the size of a dustbin lid, and getting smaller, but Carla's legs still thrashed around as she tried to get out. One of her large rubbery feet accidentally struck him in the head, and Nelson grabbed it to stop it from hitting him again.

'Oh, that tickles! You must let go! You must!' chuckled Auntie Carla.

'Get out! Get out!' were the words Nelson could hear screaming in his head, but he could not get past his auntie's massive leg in time, and the hole closed like a cigar cutter just below her knee.

There was a pop as the bottom of Auntie Carla's jelly leg was separated from the top half, and then complete darkness.

As the ground closed above him, poor Nelson realized he had not only lost his sister but he had also taken his very last breath.

THE LIGHT IN THE DARK

Some people who have experienced a close shave with death talk about seeing a light and heading towards it. And this is precisely what happened to Nelson.

As Nelson began to lose consciousness, through the dark water came a tiny light that grew and grew until it was almost blindingly bright. But there wasn't just one light. There were more approaching, above and below him too, and it seemed to be vast down here – much bigger than the surface of the small pool had suggested. As the lights drifted closer, Nelson could see that they

belonged to various kinds of fish, all with glowing scales, and though they looked a lot like the creatures that had evolved into the jelly freaks, these fish did not have the same soulless eyes. Their eyes were bright and clear and they looked right at Nelson, who looked right back at them in astonishment.

It was at this moment that Nelson asked himself a very good question.

'How come I can breathe underwater?'

It was true. Nelson was breathing. He looked down at his trainers, which he could feel slipping off his feet. The lights from the fish illuminated the water enough for him to see his shoes floating away and revealing not feet, but two green flippers.

His T-shirt billowed around him and Nelson saw that his stomach was covered in scales and his hands were fins.

As if failing to save his sister wasn't bad enough, he was now going to spend the rest of his life as a fish-shaped boy. He couldn't see his own head, but it looked something like this.

This was, after all, the River of Life. Anything that left the river evolved into something new, and it worked the other way too. Nelson was devolving, just as Carla had all those years ago.

Though Nelson was new to life as a fish, it seemed to him that he was welcomed by the luminous creatures. And he was right. As far as the fish were concerned, this little boy was a hero. For ten years their precious water had been poisoned by that wretched woman, and anyone who drank it fell under her spell. Now she was gone, the water was back to being the pure source of all life once again. They owed this boy their gratitude, so they nudged Nelson and invited him to follow them.

In the past, Nelson had always resisted making friends. He'd always felt awkward and unsure about making the commitment, but now he had a simple choice: stay in the dark on his own or follow the light being offered.

Nelson chose the light.

THE GIFT

As they sank deeper and deeper, Nelson remembered a biology lesson that covered the topic of fishes' gills and the way they are able to extract oxygen from water. Though he could not see his own face, Nelson could feel a very pleasing rush of water passing through the sides of his face and assumed that this was his new set of gills in action.

His brain was so busy dealing with this bizarre situation that for the first time since his journey began Nelson wasn't thinking of his sister or even of his monsters.

Down and down they went. As he contemplated his new body and the new life he was going to have down here in the dark, Nelson noticed that the cold water had got a lot warmer. In fact, the deeper they swam, the more it was like swimming in bath water.

It was quite a shock to suddenly see the bottom of the river. The lights from the fish illuminated the white sand and rocks and Nelson was reminded of photographs he had seen of the surface of the moon. It was so hot down here now that Nelson would have wiped his brow if he'd had one. His fellow fish skimmed the riverbed, their beautiful silver bodies gliding between mini-volcanoes that sent small jets of white sulphur into the water. Nelson found the water around him brightening and turned to see that he and his new friends had been joined by more fish.

They were now gathering around a white stone cone that rose from the riverbed and spouted white dust into the water.

Nelson found a place among the circling fish and waited eagerly to see what happened next. Maybe they were about to have dinner. Nelson realized that he was hungry, but he had no idea what kind of food he was going to eat now that he was half boy, half fish.

More than a hundred fish had assembled and after nearly a minute of silence, one of the fish swam forward and approached the mouth of the little volcano. The fish's body was long and thin like a barracuda, but its tail was as beautiful as a butterfly wing and its teeth were small and delicate.

The pretty fish swam into the cloud of white before flipping over and darting down into the volcano. It had vanished, and in doing so it had stemmed the flow of white dust. Nelson was amazed, but seconds later the pretty fish emerged from the mouth of the volcano, accompanied by a puff of white. Nelson would have clapped, but his flippers weren't much use in that department.

All eyes followed the pretty fish as it made its way towards Nelson.

I hope I don't have to do that now, he thought. He had had enough adventures for one day and swimming to the bottom of a boiling hot mini-volcano did not appeal.

It was only as the pretty fish drew nearer that Nelson realized it was carrying something in its flippers, something that Nelson recognized at once.

A Bang Stone. Fizzing and shaking just like the one he'd seen Nosh eat.

The fish wanted him to have it. And instinctively he knew why. The stone was their way of saying, 'Thanks for getting rid of that horrible whale woman and restoring paradise.'

The Bang Stone wasn't just a gift though. It was a way out. The ground above was sealed, perhaps forever, but this stone could take him wherever he wanted to go. The fish pressed in around Nelson, eager for him to eat the stone. He wanted to thank them. He wanted to let them know how grateful he was. All he could do was look around at their wondrous faces and hope that his own face somehow showed how he felt inside.

Nelson lifted the stone and opened his mouth . . .

At that very second, every single fish around him vanished with a flick of its tail, plunging Nelson back into darkness once more.

Nosh had explained how it worked: you simply swallowed the stone, thought of where you wanted to go and you would go there.

Nelson knew exactly where he wanted to go, and without hesitating he swallowed the Bang Stone, closed his eyes – and thought of his home.

The fish had done well to swim away as seconds later there was an explosion as Nelson disappeared. The riverbed erupted in a cloud of white dust that would take three days to settle, but Nelson never heard a bang or even felt a twitch.

OMMMMMMMMMM

The time it took for Nelson to travel from the riverbed to his destination was less than a heartbeat, and for that split second in time, Nelson felt every part of himself connecting with every single part of the universe. Nelson had been a boy for almost all his life, and more recently a sort of half fish, half boy, but now he was dissolving into nothing and yet at the same time becoming part of everything. He was reduced to his very essence, which he now realized was his soul. Nelson didn't just feel it and know it, he could hear it. The hum of the universe. Like the sound that's left over after a gong has been struck. Ommm. This was the sound of everything, from a rock to a rock star. It was the sound of the soul.

Everything had suddenly become so clear to Nelson that he realized he had made a mistake in where he had chosen to go. And in that fleeting moment of time, he redirected himself.

BANG!

Nelson appeared in the very same spot a jelly freak was standing, and the explosion blew the nasty fellow to bits.

He was back on the monster battlefield, only metres away from his sister, who lay lifeless in the grass. Though his vision was blurry, Nelson could see the cows running away, startled by his sudden and very noisy appearance. He felt his stomach retch and the fizzing Bang Stone pop out of his mouth. But he couldn't breathe. He gasped and remembered he was half fish! Nelson used all the strength he had left inside him to flip his body, inch by inch, towards his sister's body.

Meanwhile, his seven monsters had been winning the battle and only three of the jelly freaks were left. The rest lay twisted and broken on the beautiful ground, which was busy absorbing their bodies and replacing them with stunning flowers and ferns. The fire that had raged through the treetops was now nothing more than a few cinders.

The deadly seven were more like the messed-up seven now. Nosh lay on his back, unable to digest anything

248

more, smoke billowing from his gigantic mouth. Spike had fallen to his knees as every needle in his body had been spent and he leaked water from every open pore. Miser had lost several tentacles, but despite the pain had managed to fight on with his remaining limbs. Puff was high up in a tree, tossed there like a toy by one of the jelly freaks, and pinned beneath him was Hoot, who had got his head stuck while trying to escape earlier. The last of the deadly seven still fighting were Stan and Crush. Stan's red body was black and blue, and one of his eyes was swollen shut.

The only one in any state to fight was Crush, and he dispatched the last three jelly freaks by lashing them together with his chain-like arms and then using his head as a hammer to pound them to bits.

Carla lay gazing dreamily at the blue sky above. Nothing could dent her happiness. She didn't even care that she was now missing the lower part of her right leg. Her transformation back to the beautiful woman she had been before the fire was complete. In many ways it was a shame that, after all she had been through, Carla was about to be crushed like an ant.

'CRUSH! NO!!' shouted Nelson. Crush froze with his elephant-sized foot in mid-air, just about to bring it down on Carla's head.

All the monsters turned to see a half fish, half boy kneeling beside Celeste with his flipper hands raised above his head. Dazed, injured and exhausted, the monsters could only pant and stare as the fish-boy addressed them.

'It's me! Nelson. Don't kill her, OK? She's not a threat to you or to anyone else any more!'

The monsters said nothing.

Nelson squeezed the water from his T-shirt on to his sister's face. The journey from the riverbed to her side had given him a sense of clarity he had never felt before. It was as if his mind had always been a bin overflowing with rubbish and now it was a glass of water. And water would save his sister. The River of Life might have closed up forever, but he hoped there was still enough of it soaked into his T-shirt to revive her.

He squeezed his T-shirt as best he could with his fish flippers and wiped as much of the water as he could on to her lips until every last drop had been wrung out. All the time he was becoming less fish and more boy. By the time he had finished, Nelson had fingers and feet, and when he laid his head on her chest he knew he had ears, because he was rewarded with the greatest sound he had ever heard.

A heartbeat.

Celeste was alive! Tears filled Nelson's eyes as he cradled his sister's head and wiped the hair away from her forehead. When he looked up, Nosh, Spike, Crush, Miser, Puff, Stan and Hoot were back to their original selves, except for their battle scars. They said nothing, only smiled. When you feel this happy words are pretty useless. Celeste was alive and the ache that had tormented them since Nelson brought them into existence was gone at last.

Phew.

THE ADMIRABLE NELSON

This glorious moment was broken by the sound of sirens as a police helicopter flew over the trees, circling back when the pilot spotted the clearing in the jungle.

Nelson sprang up and began waving his arms wildly.

'Stop!' shouted Puff, who spoke so rarely, and the rest of the monsters remained silent as he continued, 'I . . . wouldn't do that . . . if I . . . were you . . . Nelson . . . how will you . . . explain . . . being . . . here?'

Nelson suddenly understood. If he was discovered by his sister's side he'd have to tell the police how he'd got here, and that could lead to terrible trouble. After all, he had driven a van illegally, stolen the identity of a woman who was currently snoozing in a toilet air-conditioning unit and before that he'd set off a fireball in Heathrow Airport. Not to mention his part in knocking out Uncle Brian.

Maybe people would believe him, but that was not a risk Nelson needed to take. He addressed the monsters (and the seven cows) as quickly as he possibly could.

'She's going to be all right now, she's safe, but Puff's right – if we stay, it'll ruin everything.'

'Master Nelson is correct. We must leave before they find us,' said Miser.

Nelson stood up and carried the Bang Stone a safe distance away from his sister. The seven monsters clustered around him and prepared to go home.

'Wot? We just gonna leave Celeste 'ere?' asked Stan.

Celeste yawned.

'Master Stan makes a valid point,' said Miser. 'One of us should remain to ensure her safety.'

The monsters looked at each other in silence. Nelson knew Miser was right, but leaving any one of his monsters alone here was a very big deal indeed.

'HONK!' said Crush, letting go of Nelson's leg and running towards Celeste, where he sat beside her head and honked again triumphantly.

'Thank you, Crush,' said Nelson, and Crush honked back, hugging Celeste's arm.

'Nosh stay wiv Crush!' said Nosh, proudly taking his place by Crush's side.

'Well, you two idiots won't make it back on yer own,' sighed Stan, striding over to join them.

'Oh, great, now we all have to feel bad for not staying with Crush,' moaned Spike, but none of the other monsters paid any attention. They had all joined Crush.

'Master Nelson, we shall watch out for her and see that she is safe,' said Miser.

Spike shrugged, sighed and joined his fellow monsters.

'Will you be able to get home again?' asked Nelson.

'We possess another Bang Stone, do we not?' said Miser, turning to see where it might be.

The other monsters looked around, but all they saw were flowers.

'It must be 'ere somewhere,' growled Stan.

'What if you can't find it?' said Nelson, and the monsters fell silent at what was clearly a very likely outcome, given the plants continuing to spring up around them.

'We do it da old-fashioned way,' said Nosh with a big grin on his face.

'Ah, yes. We close our eyes . . .' said Miser, and all of the monster closed their eyes '. . . and we all say your name.'

'Nelson.'

All seven monsters stood around Celeste pointing at Nelson and humming like bees.

Nelson felt his skin prickle and a wave of certainty fill his heart just as the pendant used to do.

'See you soon then,' said Nelson, in a wobbly little voice due to a lump that had risen in his throat.

Up in the helicopter, the pilot addressed his passenger.

'Hey! You sure this is the place?'

'Yes, this is it – but it's changed. It hasn't looked like this in ten years,' said Brian, clinging to the window rail with his good arm (the other was in a sling and his head was wrapped in bandages). Brian could see Celeste among the flowers and, a few metres away, his beloved

Carla, waving calmly up at him. For a moment he thought he saw the boy called Nelson . . .

BANG!

Nelson fell forward, partly because of the shock of being in a new place and partly because of the driving rain that blasted out of the stormy London skies. He hit the road hard with his palms, and the stone shot out of his mouth and rattled its way towards an open drain. He reached out but it was too late – the stone was carried away by the rainwater – gone forever. Nelson blinked the water from his eyes and, as he got to his feet, was suddenly bathed in blinding white light.

Uncle Pogo had never woken from a sleep with such a heavy feeling in his bones. Come to think of it, he didn't even remember going to bed. As he rolled his aching shoulders, Pogo had a vague memory of sitting down to eat fish and chips with his nephew. After that, it was all a blur. What's more, his leg was missing.

Uncle Pogo slipped into his canary-yellow dressing gown and hopped up the stairs to answer the door.

Whoever is ringing the bell must be pretty desperate, thought Uncle Pogo as he unlocked the door.

'Nelson! What on earth are you doing out there in the rain?' he said, ushering his nephew inside.

'I went out to . . . er . . . get milk.' said Nelson, as his uncle threw him a beach towel.

'Without shoes on?'

'I forgot them,' said Nelson, suddenly remembering the sight of his feet turning into flippers and his trainers floating away.

'You really are like me, aren't yer, lad?' said Uncle Pogo, chuckling as he made his way to the kitchen to make them both a nice cup of tea.

THREE WEEKS, FOUR DAYS,

FIFTEEN HOURS AND EIGHTEEN MINUTES LATER

Snip. Snip. Snip.

Nelson's eyes were shut and he felt a shiver as the scissors closed right beside his ear and a lock of his wet hair landed on his bare shoulder.

Snip. Snip.

Nelson made a shape with his mouth like a grumpy camel and puffed away the itchy little hairs that had settled on his nose.

Snip. Snip.

'You've changed,' said Celeste, her words muffled due to having a comb clenched between her teeth.

'I haven't changed,' said Nelson, although if he'd been specific he would have said, 'Nothing's changed.'

What was most incredible to Nelson was how quickly normality had resumed. Just about everything in his life had gone back to the way it was with the speed and snap of an elastic band. Homework still needed to be finished before Monday. Bins needed putting out on Wednesday. Minty wheezed and farted her days away on the kitchen floor.

It was like none of it ever happened.

Nelson wished he had a souvenir from his journey, something to remind him that it really did happen. A good scar, something small but cool just above his eye, would have been perfect. The red dots that had appeared on his back when he fell on the soul-extracting table were gone. He really had created seven monsters, and together they really had flown halfway around the world to save his sister. He had pretended to be a high-powered businesswoman and flown first class to Brazil. He had ridden a bull. He had seen his Auntie Carla transform from a nasty aquatic creature into a happy one-legged woman. A poisoned jungle transformed back into paradise. Monsters had battled each other. He had turned into a fish. He had exploded. And, for a brief moment, he had even glimpsed the very meaning of life.

But all of this was just a memory now. A memory that was so at odds with the present that it was like remembering bits of a film you had watched while half asleep on the sofa, rather than something that had really happened.

Snip. Sssnip.

He had considered telling everyone the truth, but every time the words had begun to form in his head he realized how crazy it all sounded, and maybe now wasn't a good time. The longer he left it, the less he felt the need to claim his part as the real hero in this story. He didn't even feel like a hero. He just felt . . . normal.

'Well, I heard you're going to be in Katy Newman's new play,' said Celeste.

Apart from Katy Newman there had been zero interest in his return to school. Everyone was focused on Celeste, although she had no memory of her kidnapping beyond being on the boat with her friends in Spain, so her story was always short: kidnapped by her aunt and uncle and woke up in a Brazilian jungle.

The papers had reported Carla's claims about magic and exploding stones, but who on earth was going to believe her? She was just a crazy lady who clearly lived in a fantasy world.

Katy Newman had been the only one to show any interest in Nelson. On his fourth day she accosted him in the lunch queue.

'I've written a new play. It's about the final moments before the world ends. And I need someone to be the hero.' Nelson realized she was asking him to be in her play, which he knew for a fact would be terrible, and that if he agreed to it, she would make him dress up in something embarrassing and probably even sing.

Katy's expression of hope and longing suddenly reminded Nelson of the strange fish that he had followed into the dark to the bottom of the river.

'I'll be in it, if you like,' said Nelson, and it was worth it to see Katy Newman blush before dashing away, just like the fish had done before he had exploded.

*

He was right about the play. It turned out to be her worst yet. But Nelson enjoyed being part of it nonetheless. He liked being backstage for rehearsal at lunchtime instead of kicking a ball by himself in the playground. He liked helping to build Katy's ridiculous props and learning how to make the lights different colours.

'Where's your freckle gone?' asked Celeste, and Nelson opened his eyes to see his big sister looking at him with her head tilted to one side.

'What do you mean?' asked Nelson, and Celeste handed him a tiny travel mirror so that he could see his reflection.

It was true. His one freckle that used to live right on the tip of his nose had gone.

'See, you *have* changed,' said Celeste as she admired the new short haircut she'd given her brother.

'Well, maybe just a little bit,' said Nelson.

'Lunch is ready!' shouted their father, and Nelson felt his belly rumble expectantly.

Although Sunday dinner had been an extra-lively affair due to having Uncle Pogo and his new best friend Doody to join them, Nelson had remained quiet at the end of the table.

'What's wrong with you, grumpy face?' said his mum, and Nelson sighed. It had been more than four weeks since he'd returned from Brazil and there had not been a single sign of his seven monsters. Some nights Nelson would hear a howl in the garden and rush to the window, only to discover a fox raiding their bins. Sometimes he thought he saw a monster face in the bushes at the far end of the school playground, but it was just his mind playing tricks on him. Nelson began to wonder if he had dreamed the whole thing.

As his father filled their guests' glasses with wine and they all tucked into roast lamb, Pogo and Doody told them about their new joint project. After his recent appearance on the news, TV executives had been taken by Doody's infectious enthusiasm for history and had commissioned a six-part show: *Doody Investigates!* Each week, Doody would be testing out the strange devices and gizmos they had discovered in Wren's secret chambers, and he had roped Pogo in to help him with rebuilding the apparatus that had perished.

'When I saw what this big bloke can do with a false leg – all them gadgets and gizmos – I was, like, I gotta 'ave that bloke on my team! 'E's a nutter, inn'e?' said Doody before stuffing an obscene amount of food into his mouth.

'I'm building a new leg at the moment,' said Pogo, lifting his trousers to show a new silver prosthetic limb. 'I still can't find the old one.'

Nelson's heart gave a great jolt.

He had completely forgotten about his uncle's false leg.

He'd left it with his monsters!

Nelson was so overcome with excitement that he choked and spat the food out of his mouth.

'Nelson Green! What is wrong with you!' barked his mother, but Nelson was already out of the kitchen and climbing the stairs.

He burst through the door to the spare room like a policeman about to pounce on a criminal, slammed the door shut and pushed an old armchair against the door.

Then he picked up the phone and scrolled through the contacts until he found Uncle Pogo's mobile number and pressed CALL.

There was silence except for bursts of muffled laughter from the kitchen below.

Nelson could hardly breathe. He wanted nothing more than to hear the voices of his monsters. To know they were coming back to find him. There was a click and then Nelson heard a ringtone. It was a foreign tone, which meant the false leg was still somewhere abroad.

Ring. Ring. Ring.

'Pick up, pick up, pick up,' whispered Nelson, and there was click followed by a voice speaking.

'This is Pogo. I'm sorry I can't take your call at the moment, but please leave a message after the beep and I'll get right back to you . . . BEEP!'

Nelson hung up, and at that very same moment there was a knock at the door.

'Nelson?' said Celeste. 'Are you all right?'

'Yeah, I'm fine. Just looking for something.'

'By the way, have you still got my pendant?' said Celeste.

The urge to tell Celeste the truth was impossible to resist. He was certain she would believe that he had fed it to Carla in order to save her, but as Nelson tried to think how to start, his sister spoke.

'You've lost it, haven't you?'

'Well, yeah, but I didn't mean to. It's because—'

'Don't worry,' said Celeste. 'It was only a pendant. I can get another one.' And with that, she turned and left.

Nelson took one last look out at the garden. The sun was setting behind the houses on the other side of the fence. It was a pretty sight, but Nelson felt nothing but sadness. He hadn't realized how much he missed his monster friends until now. He gave a great sniff and double blink to stop the tears that were trying to get out of his eyes, dragged the chair away from the door and joined the rest of his family, who were laughing at one of his mother's rude jokes in the kitchen.

THE QUEEN OF ENGLAND

It had been a very successful royal visit. For once her husband had not said a single thing to embarrass her. The weather had been gorgeous and her choice of hats had suited every occasion better than she'd hoped. The prime minister of Brazil had turned out to be rather more handsome in real life than the photos she had seen, and the banquet last night had been one of the jolliest she had attended in years. Once she was sure there were no more press photographers in the vicinity, Queen Elizabeth kicked off her neat white shoes and flexed her royal toes against the carpeted floor of their private plane.

A gin and tonic sat beside her, and her husband was already sound asleep in his seat.

Bliss, thought Queen Elizabeth as the plane rolled back from its stand at Rio airport and began its journey to the runway. Through the little round window she could see hundreds of people waving British and Brazilian flags and the distant flash of camera phones getting one last snap of the royal plane before it returned to London. The Queen waved back, even though no one would have been able to see her. Old habits die hard.

This would turn out to be the only part of the journey home the Queen would enjoy, for not only did it transpire that all the royal food, apart from the peanuts, had mysteriously vanished, but they would also experience random bouts of turbulence all the way home, which even the highly trained royal pilot could not explain. Queen Elizabeth would never know that it wasn't turbulence that shook her plane so wildly. It was all due to a gang of deadly monsters in the cargo hold celebrating their return to England in true monster style – although one of them had been stupid enough to fall for the same old trick and was having to fly alongside the plane, his gold feathers glinting in the sun as he hovered in the slipstream of the royal jet.

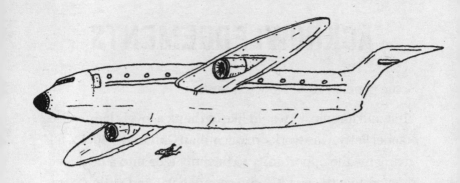

ACKNOWLEDGEMENTS

Some people I would like to thank:

First and foremost I would like to thank a lovely lady called Rachel Petty, who works at Macmillan Children's Books, for giving me the opportunity to turn my idea into a book and then editing the results with so much wit and enthusiasm. Next I want to thank a tall and brilliant American man called Frank Wuliger from The Gersh Agency and a shorter but equally brilliant British lady called Felicity Rubenstein from Lutyens & Rubinstein Literary Agency for their guidance and encouragement. A very big thank you to the entire team at Macmillan Children's Books – especially Kat and Bea – a more welcoming, talented and supportive group of human beings is impossible to imagine. I would like to apologize to my sons, Oscar, Leo, Caspar and Asa, for spending so many weekends at my desk writing when they really wanted me to go outside and play frisbee. And finally I would like to thank my wife, Louise, but I won't because she would probably be very embarrassed if I told you just how wonderful I think she is.

Some people I am definitely *not* going to thank:

I would definitely not like to thank the guy who lets his dog go to the loo right outside our front door all the time, the person who stole Oscar's bicycle and whoever it is that hides one really disgusting pistachio nut in every pack I buy.